THE SOUL OF ALL GREAT DESIGNS

THE SOUL OF ALL GREAT DESIGNS

A novel

Neil Bissoondath

Cormorant Books

Canada Council   **Conseil des Arts**
for the Arts   **du Canada**

The publisher gratefully acknowledges the support of the
Canada Council for the Arts and the Ontario Arts Council
for its publishing program. We acknowledge the financial support
of the Government of Canada through the Book Publishing
Industry Development Program (BPIDP) for our publishing activities.

Printed and bound in Canada

LIBRARY AND ARCHIVES CANADA CATALOGUING IN PUBLICATION

Bissoondath, Neil, 1955–
The soul of all great designs / Neil Bissoondath.

ISBN 978-1-897151-32-7

I. Title.

PS8553.I8775S69 2008   C813'.54   C2008-903728-6

Cover design: Angel Guerra/Archetype
Text design: Tannice Goddard/Soul Oasis Networking
Front cover image: © moodboard / Corbis
Printer: Friesens

CORMORANT BOOKS INC.
215 SPADINA AVENUE, STUDIO 230, TORONTO, ON CANADA M5T 2C7
www.cormorantbooks.com

 **Mixed Sources**
www.fsc.org Cert no. SW-COC-1271
© 1996 Forest Stewardship Council
FSC

For Anne
who reminds me that life is an adventure

and

for Élyssa
who brings her own special sparkle to that adventure

"*Secrecy has been well termed the soul of all great designs. Perhaps more has been effected by concealing our own intentions, than by discovering those of our enemy.*"

CALEB C. COLTON, ENGLISH CLERGYMAN, 1781–1832

Part One

Everybody has secrets. I have a secret. Don't you? Deep down, in your heart of hearts, as they say?

Of course you do. That pack of gum you lifted from the corner store, the beer you guzzled one summer afternoon in a corner of the basement, the porn magazine you kept stashed under your mattress to brighten up your dull evenings. How about the income you never declared, the degree you bought over the Internet, the one-night stand you never told your spouse about?

Secrets. We all have them. They're our postcards from hell — postcards we never mail, souvenirs of dark trips we mount on the interior walls of our lives, part of the hidden tapestry, so to speak. Some secrets we create, others come to us. Small or big, they're secrets all the same and we live in mortal fear of anyone ever finding them. The most important rule in life is: Don't get caught.

And yet there's something deeply unsatisfying, even sad, about having a secret that, if successfully kept, dies with you. It's as if it never existed. There's this strange urge to leave it behind, an unusual heritage. I get a thrill from imagining people reacting to the news: eyes widening in incredulity, lips parting in disbelief, perhaps the fall of a stunned *wow*.

Secrets make the world go round because, if they all came out, the world would fall apart.

Wouldn't it?

TO SEE ME you wouldn't think I have secrets of any consequence. Seeing that, in my late thirties, I dress well and have no one in my life, you might think that I lead a somewhat hermetic existence: books perhaps, classical music, a light-filled penthouse overlooking the lake, full of pastel walls and tasteful decorations. You might imagine sherry in a crystal decanter, a shiny espresso machine in the kitchen. You might throw in a Siamese cat. On a more intimate level, you might imagine the occasional bout of masturbation to keep the pipes in good working order, but nothing more passionate from this tall, bony man with slightly hunched shoulders, short brown hair and grey eyes too large for his oblong face. You might think — seeing that my gestures and my speech and my finely manicured hands suggest a certain femininity — that my tastes do not run to women. Certainly, that's what most of my clients think.

You might presume all of this but you would be wrong — about the penthouse, the music, the books, the espresso machine, the masturbation, the sexual orientation, and especially the cat. Your overall impression, however, would not be wrong. My manner is meant to encourage trust on the part of my clients, the trust they must have in their interior decorator, a trust that arises from their own gently held prejudices. In my line of work, gayness — or what many conceive to be its manifestations — confers confidence. It is one of my secrets.

PEOPLE HAVE ALWAYS been wrong about me. Before I was ten, my mother, eyeing my hands, enrolled me in piano lessons at the conservatory, three years of agony until the teachers gently broke the news that pianist's hands do not a pianist make. Later on, seeing me grow into his height and my mother's slenderness, my father prevailed on the high-school coach to enrol me in high jumping. Towards the end of my first season, I was lucky enough to dislocate a shoulder and break a leg all in one go. My father silently gave up his dreams of world championships and Olympic glory.

During the weeks of convalescence that followed, my literature teacher kept supplying me with books — to help pass the time, she said. But I knew there was more to it than that. Earlier in the term, she'd given us a writing assignment, a short story. I copied out a story from one of my mother's old women's magazines about a boy who hated his mother for thinking he was a genius. The teacher knew the story of the piano lessons. She thought I was writing about myself. She read the story to the class. The books, which she would drop off on her way home from school, were to encourage my talent. I returned them unread and I remember her disappointment at the end of the year — the way the light in her eyes seemed to blink out, leaving them tired and discouraged — when I told her I was thinking of studying electrical engineering. It was a cruel thing to do but it taught me how important people's illusions are to them, it showed me how illusions make them vulnerable. They would be happier to have their money stolen.

It was during this time of restricted mobility that I discovered my interest in interior decorating, although I wouldn't have called it that at the time. I was already interested in cars, particularly in restoring old ones. A TV documentary had caught my eye, something about the quiet fervour of the restorers — something in the way the cars spoke to them, through shape, through touch. These were not just pretty objects of machined metal. They were links to another era, when beauty was as important as efficiency and not just an aspect of marketing. Power and sensuality were reflected in the flawless body, the shiny chrome, the creamy leather seats. I was impressed by the before and after pictures: by how passion and judiciousness could resurrect elegance.

My attempts at hobbies had never survived long. For a while I built model airplanes. Spitfires and Hurricanes and Superfortresses competed for space on my bedroom bookshelves with Stukas and Heinkels and Messerschmitts, but after a time there was no tarmac space left and, worse, nothing to do with them besides dusting. I gave them up. Stamp collecting, promising for a while, ultimately failed me through its passiveness: buy, lick, stick. Then what? The television documentary offered me a new possibility: to take something that was old and rusted and broken down, bring it back to life with painstaking care, then use it. I was dazzled.

When my father came home from work I told him about what I had seen. Sitting wearily at the kitchen table, his unshaven cheeks bracketed in his hands, he said, "So, if I get this right, you want to buy some old jalopy, slap on a coat of paint, pump up the tires and fiddle with the engine."

"There's a lot more to it than that, Dad."

"You're not even old enough to drive."

I was fourteen or fifteen at the time. "I will be."

"And where do you plan on getting the money?"

"I have a job."

"You think delivering papers will pay for all this? And where do you plan on putting this jalopy of yours? If you think I'm giving up the garage, you've got another think coming."

"But Dad —"

"Don't 'But Dad' your father," my mother called from the stove where she was frying pork chops. "Go wash your hands for dinner."

Furious, I went instead to my room. How could they be expected to understand? Dad spent long, sweaty shifts on an assembly line fitting passenger doors to the carcasses of new cars, one door after another on frames which, farther down the line, would become luxury sedans he couldn't afford. Mom spent her days dusting, vacuuming and gossiping with her friends on the phone. I was amazed that they'd once shared enough passion to conceive me — or was it a matter of sheer horniness, a brief surrender to impulse that changes a life forever? My parents, it seemed to me, were people to whom life happened.

Stretched out on my bed, the last light of the setting summer sun streaming in through the window, I suddenly saw how ugly my room was. It was as if I'd never seen it before, probably because it had always been my room, changes accruing slowly, with no rhyme or reason save my changing needs. Crib to bed, table to desk, small dresser to larger dresser. The bookshelves, planks of wood supported by metal brackets screwed into the wall, had been mounted when I began school. Apart from the model airplanes, they held only a stack of textbooks. The full-length mirror beside them was added sometime later — my mother hoping that I would take more care with the way I dressed if I could see how I looked — most useful to me in checking out the size of my penis when that became a worry.

It was the colours that I found most painful. The oily-green comforter, the brown arborite desk, the melamine dresser, the royal blue mirror frame, the bookshelves slathered in egg-yolk yellow left over from an abortive attempt to prettify some garden furniture acquired at a garage sale.

Eclectic would be one word to describe what I was seeing as if for the first time. Chaotic would be another.

On the floor, a threadbare pumpkin-coloured carpet stretched wall-to-wall. To the bare feet, it was like walking on stubble. As for the walls, they had drunk no fresh paint in years. The original sky blue had grown dull and acquired a hint of dinginess from ingrained dust. No attempt had been made to clean up scuff marks or touch up scrapes. Above my desk, the wall was pockmarked with white spots where paint had peeled away with the adhesive tape I used to attach notes and photos of vintage cars. My room, I saw, resembled a rooming house for rubbies.

To be fair to my parents, I had been brought as a baby into an attractively decorated room. I've seen the photographs. But the years had brought dereliction in the way that neglect and time will slowly undo even the most exquisitely planned garden.

Almost idly, propped up on pillows on the bed, I began to speculate on how I could improve my room. Without knowing it, I had found my future.

DAYS LATER, I stripped the room clean. The desk, dresser and bookshelves were stacked on the sidewalk to await the truck from the Crips. The model airplanes were tossed into a box and donated to a home for retards. I repaired the damaged walls, sanded the baseboards, pulled up the carpet — which, to my delight, revealed a hardwood floor in decent condition. My mother, amused, agreed to sew a new cover for the comforter. My father, assured that any expenses would be paid for by my paper route, offered his tools and advice on how best to apply sandpaper, drywall compound and paint. The one thing he did himself, through fear of a botched job, was to change the light fixture on the ceiling, replacing the yellowed globe with a frosted-glass lozenge I'd picked up for a penny at a garage sale.

When it was done, my parents declared themselves impressed. I told my father that I was thinking of earning my living this way. He nodded, rubbing at his chin. "Home renovations," he said. "There's a future in that. But you have a lot to learn."

I ventured that the local community college offered a certificate in the field.

"All right," he said after a minute. "Finish high school and I'll pay the fees."

Later, my mother said, "He's relieved you've found a way to make a living. He was very worried, you know. He thought you didn't have any talent for real work."

What I never told them, and what they never found out, was that my satisfaction had come less from the physical work than from the imagining that had preceded it. Rolling on the paint was far less thrilling than the hours spent studying paint samples, mounting a variety of the little squares on each wall, observing them at different times of day, in different light, pushing my imagination to see the walls in one colour or another or in a combination of them. Sanding the baseboards was arduous compared to finding, after endless searching of garage sales and second-hand furniture dealers, just the right mirror, just the right desk, just the right dresser, refinishing them in just the right shades and positioning them in just the right spot. I began picking up decorating magazines which I stacked beneath the automobile magazines to which I subscribed. *Car &*

Driver, Architectural Digest and *House & Garden* were my pornography.

There was one more thing I never told my parents. The certificate at the college, which my father paid for and which I eventually completed with distinction, was not in home renovation but in interior decorating. There's another one of my secrets.

MY FATHER FOUND me a decent-paying job at a large hardware store. After a few tough months in the lumber yard, I was transferred to the paint section on regular day-shift. Most evenings and weekends, I worked on little contracts that came my way from a teacher at the college who owned a small consulting company advising clients on colour schemes and decorating ideas. I told my parents I was doing painting jobs to earn extra cash. From there, it seemed a simple step to dispensing decorating advice on my own.

I began discreetly slipping business cards to clients at the hardware store, offering my services. No one took me up on it. Mostly they seemed amused that a twenty-something-year-old male store clerk should be offering interior-decorating advice. After my shift, I often wandered around the parking lot picking up discarded cards, throwing out those that were damaged and pocketing for reuse those that were not. I needed a gimmick, something like those guys on TV who went to embarrassing but successful lengths to advertise their car dealerships or discount stores. But I couldn't afford TV and whatever I did had to be discreet; my father would have had a heart attack seeing me hawking interior decorating in between hockey periods.

A good businessman listens to his clients: their needs point the way towards innovation. I learned, with difficulty, I admit, to listen to the comments of those who didn't become clients.

The first time I heard the comment that would change my life — or a variation of it — was soon after I'd begun slipping cards to prospective clients. I'd helped a couple with their purchase and was moving to the next when my ear caught a whispered conversation between the woman and her husband. The woman, who was uncertain about their colour scheme, glanced at my card. She showed it to her husband. "Maybe we should give it a shot." Her husband made a face, shook his head and said, "He doesn't even look like a fag, what could he know?"

My face burned. My fists actually clenched. An angry, foolish moment. Having never played organized hockey, I wouldn't have known what to do with clenched fists. I turned away. For the rest of the afternoon, my cards remained in my shirt pocket while I, shoulders thrown back, strutted around the store like some lost lumberjack.

Twice more in the following weeks, similar comments

sent my blood pressure skyrocketing. And finally, as I was stewing in the bus on the way home, it clicked: If gay was what they wanted, gay was what they would get — on a professional level, of course.

AT THAT POINT in my life, I hadn't been around many gay men. One guy had come out in high school to muted surprise — not so much that he was gay as that he'd actually made explicit what had long been comfortably implicit — but, on the whole, to general indifference. True, a few days later he turned up with a black eye and a busted lip, but he'd had that coming anyway: despite his gentleness, he could sometimes be an arrogant son-of-a-bitch. A few clients at the hardware store had aroused my suspicions, but none of them had lisped or pranced or · flopped their wrists around.

As far as hints went, they were of no help. I thought I should do some research.

I wasn't all that familiar with the gay village. It covered a few downtown blocks east of the commercial core, a neighbourhood once known mostly for drugs and prostitution but which had been gentrified in recent years. Despite my nervousness, I couldn't help admiring the tastefully renovated row houses, the stylish bars and restaurants, the bookstores, the florist whose sweating windowpane revealed what appeared to be a tropical jungle.

I walked around for some time observing the neighbourhood, my hands stuck securely into my jeans pockets. I assumed that everyone around me was gay and was struck by how ordinary they all looked, how like everyone else: tall and short, fat and thin, clean-cut and scruffy, gregarious and reserved. Encouraged, I stopped in at a bar — bright and airy, red-brick walls adorned with bright paintings — and a little nervously ordered a beer. The man at the table beside me engaged me in a conversation about the fine, late-summer weather. His crewcut and form-fitting green T-shirt suggested the military. He stuck out his hand: "Craig," he said. Then, with no more drama than as if asking to borrow a pen, he invited me back to his place.

Stammering slightly, I said I wasn't gay.

"So what are you doing here then?"

"Having a beer." It seemed a safer answer than "Doing research."

"It's a gay bar," he said, with slight exasperation.

"Is it? I didn't know. I'm from out-of-town."

"Yeah, sure," he sneered. "Amazing how many guys from out-of-town wander into a gay bar by accident."

I guzzled my beer and stood up to go.

"Enjoy your visit, buddy," Craig said.

"Thanks, I will."

"If you change your mind ..."

The door closed behind me on the rest of his sentence.

On the subway home, once I'd got over the unsettling novelty of being the object of an attempted pick-up, I decided it was a good sign. There was hope. Sorting through my impressions, one fact stood out. The men I'd seen acting gay were fewer than those I'd seen acting macho. Reality, then, appeared to justify only one stereotype — and not the one seen most often in schoolyards, on TV and among young men eager to prove their heterosexual virility to each other. Curious how the limp wrist has become derisive shorthand for one but the gorilla grunt has not become so for the other.

This left me no further ahead, though. Slightly discouraged, I thought back on my classmate and on those clients at the store, and it seemed to me that the one quality they shared was a kind of gentleness. When I thought again about the men I'd seen and overheard in the village, even the horny, unsubtle Craig, it seemed to me that that gentleness — the gentleness of a shy person who has almost but not quite conquered his shyness — was a large part of the equation. Of course, I wasn't naive. I knew that the gay world, like the straight, had its dark corners. Graffiti sprayed onto one wall of the bar — *STRAIGHTS LIKE VINYL, GAYS LIKE ... LEATHER!!!* — had reminded me of that. But still, in both worlds, those remained dark corners.

In grade eleven I had done the set lighting for the theatre troupe at school. Sitting at the console, looking down at the stage with my earphones clamped onto my ears, I heard the drama coach say time and again, "Less is more, guys, less is more. Get it into your heads." He was talking to Romeo, whose expressions of love to Juliet were so overwrought you could see his spit showering her through the lights — and she was *above* him, on the balcony. The trick, then, was subtlety — which was well beyond our Romeo. Opening night was memorable mostly for the cry of "Jesus Christ, at last!" that rose from the back of the hall following his death scene. This need for lightness of touch also held for the lights: sunset so easily became midday with the lightest flutter of a finger. The lesson stuck with me.

By the time I kicked off my shoes at home that evening, I'd come up with a strategy: gentleness of voice, gentleness of gesture, and nothing more than that. Like the best of strategies, it was simple, straightforward and forgiving of the occasional slip-up. It'd be enough to establish suspicion without providing confirmation. All it called for was modulation, a kind of shading of my personality: trimming here, highlighting there, smoothing out the rough edges and getting the shadows — the fleeting gesture, a certain set of the lips — just right. It wasn't a question of caricature, far from that. It was, above all, a matter of internalizing a tightly held dignity.

I gave little thought to what impact all this might have on my personal life. There was no girlfriend to worry about, although I went out occasionally with some girl or other from the hardware store, usually to a movie or a student watering hole. True, it brought a level of anxiety that diminished only late at night when I was alone, with no risk of being caught out, but it was the anxiety of the game player, terrifying and exhilarating all at once. There was an art to this and, as someone, I forget who, once said, every artist is a gambler.

THE CALLS BEGAN to come, not in a great rush but with a certain regularity — choosing the new colour for a kitchen, refurbishing a den, brightening a basement, turning guest bedrooms into babies' nurseries. When my mother, noticing the increased phone traffic, remarked on all the calls I was getting, I told her they were from clients with painting jobs and from new friends I'd made at work. The next day I arranged for a phone line to be installed in my room — my dad didn't object, I was paying for it — and hooked up an answering machine that informed callers they had reached the offices of New World Design and that unfortunately all of our staff were busy at the moment but if they would be so kind as to leave a message ...

If I had any doubt as to the source of my modest success, it dissipated the day I went to visit a condominium in an expensive building overlooking the water. My former teacher had recommended me to Ian, the owner — a fairly young man, from his voice on the message. He wanted to have it all redone and was looking for the right designer. Ian wanted me to look over his place and tell him what I would do with it. I would be competing with three others for the contract — which, if I got it, would be my most lucrative by far.

I dressed carefully for the consultation in an open-necked light blue shirt, grey trousers, a blue blazer and black loafers. Here, too, modulation: professional, expensive, carefree within reason. Despite my best efforts, my mother spotted me on the way out. She whistled in admiration. "Where are you off to, dressed to kill?" I said I had a date. "Who's the lucky girl?" I told her she didn't know her, she was someone I'd met at work. "An *afternoon* date?" Kerrie — the name came to me out of the air — worked the evening shift, I said, and was free only in the afternoons. By the time my mother began voicing the next question, I was out the door.

Ian turned out to be a man in his mid-thirties with thinning hair and a voice younger than his years. He let me in, shook my hand. "Look around," he said. "Take your time and, when you're ready, speak to me as if price were no object."

"Is it?" I said.

"No."

I poked around: living room, dining room, kitchen, powder room, master bedroom and guest bedroom ensuite, a den looking out on the lake, twelve storeys below. All the walls were painted the same uninspired cream and everywhere there were furnishings bought from an outlet owned by one of those guys on television I'd once envied. For someone with imagination and an unlimited budget, it was a decorator's playground.

"The French have a word for a place that looks like this," I said. "*Affreux*." I'd picked up the word from a French-speaking client who'd used it to describe the blood-red walls in her soon-to-be-born baby's room.

He looked unfazed back at me. "So what would you do?"

"Throw out everything."

"Everything?"

"Everything."

"Even the leather chair in the den? It belonged to my grandfather."

"It doesn't go with the concept."

"The concept."

"Here, let me show you." I slid a small sketch pad from my blazer pocket and led him to the dining table. Working quickly, I sketched out the ideas that were taking shape in my brain. "These are just preliminary, you understand,"

I said. "It'll take me a few days to flesh them out. Things need time to jell."

He nodded, clearly liking what he saw, never suspecting that, with a few modifications of my own, I was essentially offering him rooms I'd seen in my decorating magazines. The concept, I said, was Mediterranean, particularly the south of France — worrying, only after I'd said it, that perhaps the south of France wasn't considered Mediterranean.

"Mediterranean," he said, as if relishing the word. He offered me a drink. We chatted, sipping at shot glasses of tequila. Ian worked in financial services for some multi-national. He travelled a great deal and had just got a big promotion, with big money. He'd decided to reward himself for all his hard work by redecorating. Then he said, "It'll be a surprise for Manuel when he finally gets his visa." Manuel worked for the Mexico City office of the multinational. They'd met at a company conference in Cancun and fallen in love. He'd been trying to get Manuel here for two years but there were immigration problems. A lawyer was working on it. Ian said, "Things other people take for granted become problems for people like us. You know what it's like, eh?"

He looked to me for confirmation. And for the first time since I'd begun applying my strategy, I slipped up, big time. Perhaps the tequila had lowered my guard. "Ian," I blurted. "I'm not gay."

"Oh." He put down his glass. "Are you sure?"

I nodded: all around me, invisible scaffolding collapsed in silence.

"I'm sorry. I thought ... You know, I thought you were family."

I capped my pen. Game over.

After a moment, he picked up his glass again, shuffled through my sketches and said, "Tell me more about your concept."

SOMETIMES, YOU'RE AWARE you're being offered a big break — the music toiler suddenly offered a recording contract, the junior lawyer suddenly given the big case. Other times, you recognize the break only in retrospect, once an opportunity has blossomed and opened up others.

Ian was my big break — or at least a good one. We agreed the work would be done while he was away on a business trip. He would be gone for two weeks. I hired two guys from the hardware to do the painting — the store supplied everything on employee discount — while I ran around town searching out the furnishings I would need to make my concept real. It was an exhausting, exhilarating time and there were moments when I despaired of getting it all done. Late one evening, I returned to the condo toting an armload of purchases to find my painters engulfed in a cloud of smoke — they took toke breaks rather than coffee breaks — and cobalt blue and sunset pink carefully applied to the wrong walls. They were not terribly concerned. When I pointed out that I'd decided on pink for the wall they'd painted blue because it was west facing and would catch the rays of the setting sun, they tried to convince me I'd mixed up my cardinal points. When one of them said with great earnestness "Who says the sun *has* to set in the fuckin' west anyways?" I understood that I'd be days fixing their mistake.

Ian returned from his trip on schedule. I was waiting anxiously for him in the condo when he arrived from the airport. He paused as he entered, set down his suitcase and peered around like a man suddenly disoriented. Then he straightened up, and his head swivelled slowly from side to side like a sunflower confused by a cloudy day. He took in the warm tones of the colours, the rustic furniture, the subtle use of wicker, the indirect lighting arranged so as to suggest the reflection of a raging sun, the handwoven rugs strewn across the parquet floors, the sprays of greenery from the potted tropical plants.

I couldn't read his expression.

Then a smile broke across his face and he said, "Manuel's going to love this."

IN THE COMING months, Ian directed several jobs my way. I redid his sister's basement, helped a couple of his friends remodel their living rooms, advised some of his colleagues' wives on colour schemes. Within half a year, I had more work than I could comfortably handle. I told my father that with so many painting jobs coming in, I was considering quitting the hardware.

Stretched out on his La-Z-Boy, nursing his pre-dinner beer, he told me I was crazy. Going out on my own was uncertain, the supply of work was unpredictable, it could dry up at any moment. The hardware store was a sure thing. If I stuck with it I was certain to be given a department manager's position. "Don't be a fool," he said.

My mother, without looking away from the TV, said, "Listen to your father, Cal. Don't give up on a sure thing. You're only twenty-five. By the time you're fifty, who knows? You might be president of the company."

I wondered whether she'd said the same thing to my father thirty years before.

It was time to move out on my own, get an apartment midtown, closer to my client base. And it was time to incorporate, to make my business real, with an office and a desk and even a receptionist. I was determined to establish a full-service company, not just interior decorating but — with an eye to long-term growth and product excellence — the workmanship as well, with reliable carpenters and plasterers and electricians and painters to execute the plans I dreamed up.

Although I had saved a fair amount of money, I would need a great deal more to get things off the ground. And I had to find a way to do it so that my clients would focus on the consulting while my parents focused on the labour.

FINDING AN APARTMENT turned out to be tougher than I'd imagined. Over the years, the city had achieved success beyond its dreams. The big, clean, safe, prosperous, slightly provincial city I'd grown up in had become immensely rich, a powerhouse of economic activity fuelled by banks, businesses, the stock exchange, major-league sports teams and the burgeoning beehive industriousness of hundreds of thousands of recent immigrants. A new energy had come to the place even as the old sense of a city that worked began to shred. Certain neighbourhoods were no longer safe after dark and policemen had to wear flak jackets while out on patrol. Now the summer light was dulled by a layer of brassy smog, the commute home took two hours rather than thirty minutes and random shootings were no longer loathsome events from distant elsewheres. All that was simply part of the price to be paid for living in a city where all manner of desire could be satisfied, where tinted-window stretch limousines prowled our streets, where the black-tie-and-evening-dress crowds shelled out hundreds of millions for cultural centres and the extravaganzas of one kind or another needed to fill them. In this new and slightly manic city, the only thing stronger than the smell of exhaust fumes was the smell of money — and it was that money, which could buy beauty, that I was going after.

I began my search in midtown, a large area chocka-block with boxy, red-brick apartment buildings from the forties and fifties, concrete behemoths from the sixties and airy glass-and-steel towers from the seventies and early eighties. Downtown, closer to the water, construction cranes scrutinized like skeletal waiters the incomplete office and condominium towers multiplying on land once preciously protected from development. The suburbs of my childhood grew even more amorphous as the city limits spread, gobbling up small towns once on its periphery with dense housing estates — palatial homes breathing down each other's necks across slivers of fenced-in lawn.

Tens of thousands of apartments, then, but vacancies were as rare as virgins at a hooker convention. For weeks I ran through the rental listings in the newspapers, making fruitless calls to complacent landlords and harried sub-letters. I did manage to get two appointments to inspect unsecured flats. In the first, the ripe malignancy of mould in the kitchen gave way to the keen virulence of shit in the bathroom. In the other, the landlady swore that a bit of elbow grease would remove the bloodstains from the scuffed living-room floor. The place would be available, she said, once the police had completed their investigation.

A new strategy was called for. With the help of the phone book, I began cold-calling the rental offices of all the midtown buildings. In every case, my inquiry was met by a curt "Nothing available" and a crisp click.

There was only one thing left to do: cold-call in person.

Over the next few days, I spent every spare moment walking from building to building talking to superintendents and managers, interludes of refuge in overheated offices from the frigid temperatures outside. But the answers, more politely offered than on the phone, still left me disheartened.

And then, late one snowy afternoon, an imminent death came to my rescue.

Christmas had come and gone in its usual desultory fashion. There was a quick exchange of gifts on Christmas morning — I gave a box of bath oils to my mother, a new tool box to my father, they gave me a pair of painting overalls, they gave each other nothing. This had been followed by a day of television (my father grumbling throughout the colourized version of Alastair Sim's *Scrooge*), which was followed by a dinner of roast beef, canned peas, mashed potatoes and chocolate cake (my mother grumbling as usual that the food had not co-operated: the beef was overdone, the potatoes were lumpy, the cake was dry).

New Year's arrived with glasses of beer and Dick Clark in Times Square.

The year was already ten days old. I'd been trudging around discouraged for the better part of an hour, my boots were damp from the wet snow and I was tempted to call it quits for the day even though there were still three buildings left to visit on the street. I was tired of asking the same question, getting the same answer, and the gloomy mid-winter afternoon did nothing to lift my spirits. Dirty buses trundled by, half-empty. Across the street, an old man slipped on a sheet of ice, tumbled to the sidewalk, slowly picked himself up, brushed his glasses clean and continued on his way.

I'd already walked past the entrance to the building when I suddenly turned back. I don't know why. I simply did, attracted perhaps by the globes of white light that sat atop the beribboned pillars flanking the polished wooden doors. It was one of those red-bricked forties buildings, with windows so small they suggested twilight interiors. I pressed the button labelled "manager" and the door buzzed and clicked in response.

The lobby, with a damp terrazzo floor, lime green walls and steel elevator doors, was not encouraging. The manager's office was off to the right. I knocked and entered at the growled invitation. A thickset, balding man looked up from behind an expansive mahogany desk. His dark suit and red tie seemed rather grand for an apartment-building manager. The single lamp on his desk left much of the office in shadow but revealed the polish of wood panelling and the glint of many photograph frames. An ornate, well-stuffed chair sat before the desk but he did not offer it.

I asked my usual question, got my usual answer. Oh, well. I turned to go.

But then he said, "You have a job?"

"I'm self-employed," I said. "I have my own company."

"Your own company! Impressive for such a young man. What kind of product does your company make, may I ask?" There was the slightest accent, just a hint of the vowels of my high-school nurse who had come from somewhere in central Europe.

"It's an interior decorating company."

"You're an interior decorator?"

"Yes."

"Business is good?"

"Good enough."

He thought for a moment. "If you're not in too much of a hurry, I might have something for you, pending a credit check of course." His palm gestured me towards the chair. "Apartment 102, ground floor. It's only a bachelor. Not very big or bright — it looks out onto the interior courtyard — but it might be coming available soon." The tenant, he explained, was an old woman who had lived alone for many years. Now she was very ill and in hospital. "Between you and me, chances are she'll croak soon. When she does, the place becomes available. Perhaps for you. If ..."

"If ...?" I'd heard about bribes being offered to building managers. I'd never been asked for a bribe before. It was unsettling.

"I'll be frank with you," he said, leaning forward at his desk and straightening his already straight tie. "Here's the situation. We operate under rent control, as you know. Part of me is sympathetic, but part of me is deeply saddened by the lack of money for maintenance. You've seen our lobby. Just think of what it could be like if I could charge fair rent and put some of that money towards beautifying the place. You're an interior decorator. Imagine what it could be like."

He was right, of course. I'd seen the main doors, I'd seen the lobby. The potential was obvious.

"So here goes." He told me the current rent and then told me what the new rent would be — a twenty percent hike, well above the increase allowed by rent control.

It was illegal but I was relieved at not having been asked for a bribe — and even more so that, while the rent was steep, it wasn't beyond my means. I took out one of my cards, placed it on his desk. "Give me a call if the place becomes available, okay?"

He plucked a form from the desk drawer. "Fill out this application form. I can run a credit check and, if you pass,

I will put you on our waiting list." He offered me the use of his fountain pen.

Two days later, a message was waiting for me on the answering machine: "The apartment has come available and will be ready for occupancy in two weeks. If you are still interested, please stop by my office tomorrow during office hours to sign the lease. Tomorrow. Please understand I cannot hold it any longer than that."

When I heard the message I had just come in from a long night and morning of working on a rush job, redoing the home office of a couple who were away skiing for a few days. His tomorrow was already my today. I was filthy, I was exhausted and a snowstorm was roaring through the city. I dialed the number he'd left and recognized his voice the moment he answered. I explained that the storm made it difficult for me to get there, could he wait until the following day?

"I'm afraid not," he said. "Company rules. You have twenty-four hours to accept or refuse an offer to rent and to sign the lease."

"All right," I said. "I accept, but can we take care of the paperwork tomorrow?"

"As I've already explained, it doesn't work that way." He paused, and I imagined him straightening that already straight tie. "But here's what I'll do. The storm is expected to pass within a few hours. I will wait for you in my office for one hour past regular office hours. If you are not here by six o'clock, I will telephone the next person on our waiting list and go home. I think that's more than fair, don't you?" Then he hung up.

I showered and dressed quickly and, drumming my fingers on the kitchen counter, waited for the coffee machine to finish its gurgling. Through the window above the kitchen sink, the storm continued driving hard, effacing the neighbouring houses that were so close my mother usually waved her friends over for mid-morning coffee. The all-news radio station — left on all day to thrill my mother with the latest news of disaster, her moments of monotony enlivened by news flashes of violent death — announced that the airport had been closed. The trip home, on a bus packed with glum passengers stewing in damp, exhausted air, had been laborious; the thought of repeating the trip back downtown was almost unbearable.

My mother, stretched out on the sofa watching a soap, called out, "Your father's home early."

He came in through the kitchen door a minute later, stamping snow from his boots and dusting it off his shoulders. Not wanting to face rush hour in the storm, he'd clocked out early from his shift. I poured us each a cup of coffee. He took his gratefully, nodding in thanks. My father had never been comfortable with driving. He'd got his licence only after being hired on at the factory, and only because the hour-and-a-half bus ride to work was cut by two-thirds. He said, "The snowplough guys'll be earning overtime tonight."

"So you won't be needing the car this evening?" I said.

He squinted at me above the rim of the coffee cup. "If she's worth driving for in this weather, she's worth marrying. Who is she?"

I hadn't told them I'd been looking for a place of my own. They wouldn't have understood. I wanted to have the lease signed and sealed before breaking the news. I said, "It's not a girl, Dad. It's a job. A big job."

"No job's that big."

"It's a whole house. One of those places overlooking the ravine."

"So it can wait till tomorrow. What's the rush?"

"I don't know. The owner's an old biddy, kind of eccentric, I guess. If I don't go sign her piece of paper this afternoon she says she'll give the job to her grandson. I really want this job, Dad."

From the living room, my mother said, "Are you out of you mind? In this weather?"

My father said, "Buses are running."

"Creeping is more like it. It'd take me hours."

He dipped his hand into his pants pocket, tossed me the keys. "Take it easy out there."

My mother said, "You're letting him have the car? I don't know who's crazier, you or him."

He twitched his eyebrows at me, a signal of tolerance

for the mother she was being. "He's not a kid anymore."

I guzzled my coffee, zipped up my parka and headed out into the pounding storm.

THE MANAGER WAS waiting for me behind his desk. The half-hour drive had taken me almost two. He was wearing the same dark suit, the same red tie. The lease was set squarely on his desk, the uncapped fountain pen lying diagonally across it. He said, "I knew you'd make it." Then he placed his palms flat down on the table. "She croaked this morning."

Three days later, the apartment stripped of the old woman's belongings, I was allowed in. It was stuffy with the smell of cats and damp litter. The white walls, whiter where framed pictures had hung for a long time, were marked in places by a tracery of fine cracks. The parquet floor was in good condition except at the front door where foot traffic had worn through the shellac to the wood. The windows, which looked out onto an inner courtyard deep with snow that would melt in spring to reveal a chaos of weeds, could be opened only a few inches; as a security precaution, short chains had been welded between them and the frames. The manager informed me that the place needed some work — a fresh coat of paint, some new plumbing in the bathroom, new wiring and appliances in the kitchen. This was the landlord's responsibility but I sensed where he was heading. Then he said it would be ready for occupancy in ten days. He was either a less calculating man than I'd thought or a more foolish one.

When I returned home later that evening, my mother had gone to bed and my father had fallen asleep in his La-Z-Boy waiting up for me. He asked how things had gone. I said I'd signed. He nodded groggily and went off to join my mother. I'd already decided that I would tell them about the apartment only when I had the keys.

Later on, when people remarked on my luck at having found a good apartment in such a terrific location, I left it at just that — luck. There was something distasteful about admitting the role a convenient death had played. It wasn't a big secret — it might even have got a laugh — but it was one I nevertheless guarded carefully.

THE EVENING OF the afternoon I first let myself into the apartment — the windows bright with sunshine, the smell of fresh paint and disinfectant overwhelming the animal mustiness present ten days earlier — I steeled myself to tell my parents I was moving out. I helped myself to a beer and joined my father in the living room. Stretched out as usual on the La-Z-Boy with his pre-dinner beer, he eyed my bottle and said, "Celebrating something?"

"Kind o'."

"You going to keep it to yourself?"

"Can we wait until Mom joins us?" She was still in the kitchen giving a final basting to the roast chicken.

"Sounds big."

"Kind o'."

He belched into his cupped palm. "Not getting married, are ya?"

"Nope."

I sprawled out on the sofa. Darkness had fallen hard outside, winter hard, as if a lid had been clamped on the world. The living room was lit only by the feeble light of a floor lamp, the way my father liked it. After the brightness and din of the factory floor, he enjoyed this dusky silence at home.

Perhaps because I was aware that I'd be leaving within a day or two, I found myself examining the living room — this room that was as it had always been, a place so familiar I'd stopped seeing it. The light green walls, the dark green carpet, the cream chintz curtains covering the picture window, the fireplace that was rarely used, the mantelpiece crowded with knickknacks meaningful only to my mother, the large, ugly oil painting of a forested mountain in winter hanging on the wall above it, the sliding glass door that led to the small backyard where, every spring, my mother planted the begonias she bought in little pots from the nursery at the shopping centre. Looking around, growing aware of the odour of desperate cleanliness that underlay that of the roasting chicken, I had a moment of fear, a kind of shudder deep in my belly. I suddenly saw that, from now on, I would be absent here, and these colours, that odour, would go on without me.

My mother padded into the living room, her frilly bedroom slippers soundless on the carpet, her beer frothing in a glass.

My father said, "We've got something to celebrate." Then he turned in my direction, as if to give me the floor.

My mother brushed my legs off the sofa and sat beside me. "So, what's going on?"

"I'm moving out," I blurted. "I've got myself a place in town."

My mother's eyes widened a little. My father paused mid-swig, his gaze settling on me for a second.

My mother said, carefully, "Where to?"

"Midtown."

My father said, "That's an expensive area."

"I can afford it. It's been under rent control for years."

My mother nodded once. "And is it a nice place?"

I described the building, the apartment.

"Sounds super," she said. She turned to my father. "That's it, then. You should give Mr. Mumford a call tomorrow morning."

"Who's Mr. Mumford?" I said.

My father gave another gentle belch. "A real estate agent."

My mother, turning back to me, said, "We've been kind of waiting for you to make this decision. We've been wanting to sell the house for some time now, move into a smaller place. We've put a down payment on a condo, a new development closer to your father's work. It's a lot smaller than the house, of course, but I'll have a lot less cleaning to do."

My father said, "And I won't need the car anymore."

I pulled myself up straight. "You've already made a down payment? When were you planning on telling me all of this?"

My mother put her hand on my knee. "We didn't say anything before because we didn't want you to feel we were pushing you out. We were hoping you'd decide to move out on your own, but we'd have stayed here as long as you wanted to."

A kind of sadness bubbled up through my surprise. I would not be the only one who would be absent here. These colours, that odour, would not go on without me after all.

The very next day the realtor's sign — Mr. Mumford himself grinning like a fat-cheeked pimp above his phone number — was planted in the snow out front.

Two days later, my father hitched a trailer to his car and helped me move into my new place. As a housewarming gift, my mother carefully packaged a set of dishes that had long sat gathering dust in the basement storage room. They had been given to her years before by departing neighbours. Then she added a set of cooking pots she'd bought on sale but never found any use for. And finally, digging through storage cartons in the garage, she came up with an almost complete set of yellow-handled cutlery.

When I protested it was too much, she said, "It'll all have to go anyway. There isn't enough room in the condo for all this junk."

"See?" my father said with a grin. "She's just given you a bunch of junk, that's all."

In the forty-eight hours since Mr. Mumford's sign had gone up, he'd acquired a vigour and an ease I hadn't seen in years.

FUNNY HOW WORD gets around. New World Design was doing well, three or four jobs a month, often more, certainly enough to keep things afloat, but I had the sense that the company wasn't growing, that it was established, but precariously. I placed a few small ads in the paper but it was mostly word of mouth — ridiculous expression, when you think about it — that brought in the work and acted as a warning to me to safeguard my persona: word of mouth was like fishing with dynamite, potent but undiscriminating. So I wasn't yet confident enough to let go of my job at the hardware. That income was a sure thing and I planned to live frugally through the remaining winter months in order to build up a nest egg which I could park safely in the bank. Once people had paid off their Christmas bills and the weather began warming up, there would be more jobs — enough, I hoped, to keep me busy full-time.

I was restocking the shelves one evening at the hardware when I got called to the manager's office. Rumours had been going around that a department manager's position was opening up and my co-workers, convinced I was about to be promoted, slapped me on the shoulder and good-naturedly sent me off with cries of "Hey, Boss" and "See you later, sir."

The manager's office was on the mezzanine overlooking the floor. I'd been up there only once before, when I first came to the job. I knocked at the door and the manager, a gaunt middle-aged man who brushed the last of his hair forward onto his forehead, opened it himself. I stepped inside and saw that the small, ordered office was crowded. Two policemen were standing beside the desk.

I thought: But I haven't done anything wrong, I haven't even pocketed a screw.

The manager said, "Take a seat, young man." He was new. I'd only seen him walking around the floor taking notes on a clipboard. I sat down on the wooden chair he nudged towards me.

One of the policemen removed his cap. "I'm Constable Saunders," he said.

Constable Saunders. I've never forgotten the name of the stranger who told me my parents were dead.

THEY HAD GONE to visit their condominium, my father overcoming his dislike of driving, particularly at night. Conditions were good, although there were icy patches on the roadway. But something had gone wrong. My father, Constable Saunders said, appeared to have lost control of the car — perhaps ice, perhaps speed, perhaps a mechanical problem ... Was my father a drinker, did he have a heart condition or something like that, was he on any medication? The investigation would tell the story. But whatever the reason, as he was negotiating a curve on the downward slope of a hill, my father swerved out of his lane and directly into the path of an oncoming car. The impact was crushing, my parents ... it would have been instantaneous. The other driver was in critical condition.

As I sat deadened, the manager placed a hand on my shoulder and asked if there was anyone he could call. I shook my head. Those members of my parents' families who wished to attend the funeral would have to fly in from out west.

Constable Saunders said, "Is there anything we can do for you?

"Yes," I said. "Tell me what kind of car it was, the one they hit."

He gave me a puzzled look. He didn't understand that I needed to know whether the car that killed my parents was one my father might have helped build on the assembly line. Had he, unwittingly and however briefly, once touched the instrument of his demise?

Constable Saunders said, "I'm sorry, I don't have that information." He glanced uneasily at his partner. "Are you sure there isn't something we can do for you?"

The manager called a taxi to take me home on company expense and assured me of two weeks fully paid bereavement leave.

THE EVENING OF my parents' funeral, the western representatives of the family and a few friends — a fistful of my father's colleagues, my mother's coffee mates (as they referred to themselves) and a scattering of neighbours with whom my parents had had intermittent social intercourse — gathered at the house. They cluttered the dining table with food, plates and cutlery, the kitchen counter with an array of alcohols, mixers, glasses and ice.

Everyone shook my hand or squeezed my shoulder or planted a brief kiss on my cheek. Then they gathered with their own in different corners of the living room, plates balanced on laps, drinks gripped in fists, and made small talk.

I stood off to one side, dredging a fork through a plate of potato salad someone had given me: *You must eat, you must keep up your strength.* I didn't really know any of these people and, even though grateful for their presence, found myself disconcerted. It was a party that couldn't quite get going — the lights were too bright, there was no music. I put down the plate and went over to the record player my parents had used only infrequently. Among the records filed beside it — Bobby Darrin, Paul Anka, Nat King Cole — I found an Elvis Presley. The condition of its jacket suggested that once it had been a favourite. I slid out the disc, put it on the turntable and watched as, at the push of a button, the arm rose and settled on the spinning vinyl.

Elvis declared that his girlfriend was nothing but a hound dog. He got no further. Someone quickly switched off the record player while someone else took me gently but firmly by the arms, directed me towards the kitchen and pressed me down into a chair.

My aunt Ella, a female version of my father as he might have looked in ten or fifteen years, took the chair beside me. Married young, she'd been widowed five years later when her husband tumbled headfirst from the top of an oil rig. She'd never remarried. Ella had come east only once before, for my parents' wedding. Now she was back, for their funeral.

She placed her hand on my knee. "I'm sorry, dear, your choice of music wasn't the best, considering. Don't you agree?"

"I thought things needed livening up a bit," I said.

She gave me a sympathetic look, the skin crinkling around her watery eyes. In the light, I could see bare scalp through her permed, too-dark hair. "Not just yet."

My uncle Peter knocked discreetly at the door frame. "Everything all right?" he said. Any resemblance he might have had to my mother was well-hidden behind a thick, greying beard. He was a high-school principal but his dark suit and self-effacing manner had caused him to appear perfectly attuned to the funeral home.

"Oh, fine," Ella said. "Just a little misunderstanding."

Peter went to the bottles on the counter. "Drink anyone?"

"Is there any whisky?" Ella said.

He hefted a bottle. "Neat or on ice?"

"Oh, neat. It's the only way."

Unscrewing the cap, he glanced at me.

"Anybody bring any wine?" I said.

He looked around. "Just red, I'm afraid. Will that do?"

As Peter prepared the drinks, Ella turned to me. "So tell me, do you have a girlfriend?"

"No." I thought it best to keep my answers short.

"No? Such a nice young man like you. There must be loads of girls out there just dying to get their hands on you."

I caught Peter's quick glance, his slight frown, his sudden, intense concentration on the corkscrew he was twisting into the bottle's neck: I knew then that he'd observed me, sized me up, drawn his conclusions. Just like my clients.

"You know," Ella said, reaching up to take the glass Peter held out to her, "young people like you ..."

As she launched into a lecture on the importance of marriage and children, the preservation of the family name, the perpetuating of my parents' memory, I found myself paying little attention, her voice becoming a kind of background flutter to the pleasures of the wine sliding down my throat and of the sight of Peter's growing agitation. Twice he made an attempt to leave the kitchen, and both times he held back: should he intervene? I began enjoying his indecisiveness, seeing his eyes trying to catch Ella's but unable to breach her expanding thesis on the role of human reproduction. When she predicted the eventual disappearance of the white race if young people like me didn't do our biological duty, Peter — looking very much like a member of the white (and whiter and ever whiter) race — finally darted from the kitchen to the living room.

Seconds later, Peter's new wife — his third — bustled in. She'd worn a gaucho outfit, complete with hat, because it was the only thing black she had in her wardrobe and there hadn't been time to shop. Earlier, assuring me that our fates were written in the stars, she'd hoped I would find comfort in knowing that the accident was simply destiny's way of letting my parents know it was checkout time.

"Ella," Petra exclaimed. "There you are! I've been looking all over for you."

Ella, unhappy about having her flow of demographic statistics interrupted, said, "It's not a very large house."

Petra yanked her up from the chair, a spray of whisky rising from Ella's glass and finding haven on my trouser leg. "Come now, honey, you've got to tell me about your house," Petra said. "I hear it's fabulous." She turned to me. "You don't mind if I steal your aunt Ella for a little while, do you, honey?" Without waiting for an answer, she hustled Ella out of the kitchen very much the way Ella had hustled me into it.

I could see them from the corner of my eye, Ella with her back to the wall, Petra whispering earnestly, Ella's palm meeting her lips in dismay, her startled glance towards the kitchen.

A little while later, my father's former colleagues came in for refills. They nodded shyly at me, helped themselves from the fridge. On the way out, one of them leaned over and whispered, "I know it's tough, kid, but go easy on the bottle, okay? Whisky's no answer." This — and the glass of cola he was drinking while the others had beer — was how I recognized Stan. He could smell Ella's spilled drink on me. My father had once said that Stan, an anti-alcohol proselytizer and long-time member of AA, hadn't grasped the full implication of the second A, and that some of the guys had been threatening to get him a dictionary.

My father had had a fondness for words, but only in crossword puzzles. He spent hours doing the newspaper ones and bought himself books full of them. Often though, when he tried to use some of his more exotic words, they didn't come out quite right. *Awry*, for instance, left his tongue as *aw-ree*, *manic as maynic*, as if they couldn't quite survive the transition from squares on paper to the breathing world. My dad was that kind of man: his worlds were small, compartmentalized, and he operated with confidence only within them.

In a burst of inspiration, I asked the guys to wait. Trotting down to the basement, I retrieved my old high-school dictionary, largely unused and only slightly musty. I held it out to Stan. "My dad always wanted you to have this," I said.

He put down his glass and took the dictionary reverentially in both hands. "For me?" he said, moved.

The others glanced over his shoulders, eyeing the gift. One by one, their faces lit up behind him. Two raised thumbs at me. One said, "Good man."

Stan frowned in puzzlement. "Why a dictionary, eh, guys?"

"That's easy," I said quickly. "He always said you were one of the smartest guys he ever knew and he thought you should read the dictionary. Starting with A. He was planning on giving it to you himself but, you know ..."

Stan sniffled and the others led him back to their corner in the living room.

When they said goodnight some time later, each squeezed my hand tightly. *He was a good guy. The best. It won't be the same on the line. Take care, guy.* Stan alone said nothing. Holding the dictionary in the crook of his left arm, he gave me a sad smile and followed the others out. Only later did I worry that I might have written my name on the inside cover.

Not long after, family members, the neighbours, the coffee mates — each clutching a cup from my mother's cupboard as a memento — congregated to say goodbye. Ella, stiff-backed, offered a perfunctory handshake and a firm, "I will pray for you." Peter and Petra were warmer: hugs, pats on the back, kisses, *Call if you need anything.*

As I closed the door behind them, a feeling of unease came to me. I realized that I preferred Ella's way. She'd made it clear where she stood. With Peter and Petra, things were less coherent. They left me with an impression of great compassion, and acceptance of whom they'd assumed me to be. But they also left me with a measure of confusion: curious as it may seem, I couldn't be sure they were sorry for me because of my parents' death or because they believed me to be gay. Most of all, though, I was struck by the realization that I hadn't been acting, not even a little. My persona — marked by that gentleness that had begun as a marketing ploy — had come naturally. I turned off the lights and went to bed, the last night I would spend in the room I'd remade in the house in which I'd grown up.

I was exhausted, but sleep did not come easily. Ella's questions about my personal life had surprised me, not because she'd asked them but because I'd never taken the time to ask them of myself. I had acquaintances, men and women, among the regulars I hired to help out on various jobs, people with whom I'd have the occasional beer or plate of chicken wings at a sports bar but the whole matter of girlfriend-spouse-children was one I'd relegated to the mental box where I filed vague notions about retirement funds and annual medical checkups. They were things which would eventually solve themselves. More than that, though, the notion of a girlfriend didn't fit with the persona I'd fashioned for myself. For the good of my business, it had to be safeguarded and nothing would be more detrimental than being seen socially in the company of a woman.

As I waited for sleep to come, I found that Ella's questions had opened up the box and pulled out a file full of longing. I contemplated it for a while, letting the ache of absence wash over me, remembering with startling clarity an encounter behind a stack of boxes in a storage room from my early days at the hardware. Clarissa from the lighting department, early forties, plumpish, with long chestnut hair and blue-green eyes. She wanted to show something to the new guy. In the murky light of the storage room, she showed me her breasts, and what pleasure her hands and mouth could offer me, and what pleasure my hands and tongue could offer her. Later I found out that Clarissa took almost every guy to the storage room, but only once. Rumour had it that when her husband picked her up at the end of her shift, she would tell him in detail about the visits to the storage room. It excited him. I tended to avoid the lighting department after that. But lying there in bed that night, remembering all that she'd shown me, I recalled most vividly the smoothness of her skin, the warmth of her flesh, the sweet scent of her hair, the firm press of her palms on my lower back. That was the memory that triggered the ache that washed over me, an ache that might have been more familiar had it not been for my exhaustion at the end of every day. I turned around in the bed, shut the file and shoved it back into the box.

My eyelids grew heavy and, through the deepening drowsiness, the new name for my company came to me. I fell asleep knowing that New World Designs was no more.

ABOUT A WEEK after the funeral, Mr. Mumford called with an offer on my parents' house. I accepted it on the spot, uppermost in my mind the need to divest myself of a past

I'd already decided to abandon. Mr. Mumford also settled the question of the down payment on the condominium, the purchase of which he'd arranged. Once he assured the construction company that he had a new buyer standing by, they agreed to a full refund less the administrative costs. My father's modest but not insubstantial life insurance came in. I was flush with money.

Some secrets resolve themselves, losing their weight, shrivelling and peeling away from that internal tapestry. They cease being secrets because those who would care no longer exist. As the shock of the loss of my parents gradually thinned, a new sense of freedom slowly germinated.

For a while, I continued receiving condolences from people whose names were little more than faint echoes to me. One day, the neighbour who'd given my mother the set of dishes now mine telephoned from two time zones away. Directory assistance had located me and she was still taken aback by the fact that the little boy she'd known all those years ago now had his own telephone number. The news of the accident had devastated her, she said, and she wanted to know if I had a brother or sister to help ease the pain of my loss. When I told her I was an only child, she told me, weeping on the phone, something I had never known: that my parents had tried hard, very hard, to have another child, they'd joked about having enough children to field a family hockey team. Sniffling, she asked how I was holding up, and as I reassured her that I was all right, that time was healing the wound, I found myself having to mute the true tenor of my feelings. My new sense of freedom, I realized, was not one I could admit to anyone. People would be horrified.

SOME WEEKS LATER, I found out that the car was made by a rival company. I also found out the cause of the accident. Something had come loose in the brake mechanism as my father attempted to slow the car on the downward curve of the hill. He would have panicked as he felt the beast he had never trusted bolt from his control. He would have given in to its wilfulness.

There would probably have been warning signs, the police mechanic said, a funny feeling in the brake that was difficult to describe, like too much sudden give in the pedal, for instance, or a kind of silent vibration, signalling a problem to the driver. But my father had never mentioned any funny feeling in the brake. To him, a car always felt funny, unnatural. The mechanic shrugged and I elected not to tell him that I knew precisely what that funny feeling was like.

I'd felt it on the drive back home after signing the lease. Wending my slow way through the clogged streets, wipers swiping the windshield free of falling snow, the steering wheel with too much play, the tires with too little purchase, maintaining distance from cars fishtailing ahead of me, I twice felt the brake pedal hurtle into what felt like nothingness for a dizzying few seconds before engaging the mechanism. Each time, I uttered a little *Shit!* to fill the skip in my heart, blaming not the car but the road conditions, ascribing the cause to packed snow or a chunk of ice that had somehow wedged itself into some vulnerable spot. Exhausted from the drive, excited at having secured the apartment, it never occurred to me to mention the brake to my father when I finally got home.

LIKE APARTMENT RENTALS, affordable office space was not easy to come by and what was available was either too hidden away or too dingy or too expensive, and sometimes all three. So it was a matter of luck that walking home late one damp spring evening, I happened upon movers carting furniture and filing cabinets from an office building not far from my apartment. On impulse, I asked whether the space they were emptying had been rented. They didn't know, but since it was a bankruptcy, chances were good that no one had yet snapped it up. I scribbled down the name of the holding company. By the following afternoon, I'd signed the lease.

There was more space than I needed. Four offices surrounded a spacious reception area carpeted in grey. Pinned to the lime green walls were two travel posters touting the pleasures of Costa Rica. Two of the offices overlooked the street, the other two the parking lot. One I would use for storage, another for planning sessions with clients, the third would remain empty for the moment, and the fourth I would convert into my office. I would've preferred a street view but I felt that clients walking through the aluminium-and-glass main door would be reassured by the sight of someone beyond a receptionist. A sense of desertion, of inactivity, would be discouraging.

Over the following weeks, while the lawyer who had handled my parents' affairs took care of the legal paperwork, I transformed the place. The grey carpet was replaced by a royal blue one, the fluorescent fixtures by accent lights camouflaged in lush potted trees, the lime green of the walls by the subtle hues — greys, pinks, blues — of a late summer sunset. I cut full-page photos from decorating magazines, had them framed and hung them around the reception area. An old stereo, a hundred feet of speaker wire and two discreet speakers filled the background with soft rock.

I shopped around for deals on furniture — I refused to contemplate the chrome-and-cream tubular carcasses from office suppliers — and gradually, through garage and bankruptcy sales, stock liquidations and second-hand dealers, put together a set of elegant, eclectic furnishings. The most expensive item, bought brand new, was a black espresso machine.

Through the university student-employment office, I found a part-time receptionist, three hours a day, five days a week. I was being cautious with expenses and, since potential clients tended to call between 10:00 a.m. and 2:00 p.m., I saw no need to pay for more. Anyone calling outside of those hours would get either me — *Please hold for a moment while I transfer you* — or the answering machine. It was not spectacular — spectacular would come later — but it was tasteful, understated and, most important of all, did minimal damage to my bank balance.

Prudent, I'd locked away most of the money that had come to me, investing what I thought an adequate sum in the company and depositing six months of apartment rent in a separate chequing account. Work continued trickling in, but at no greater volume than before. Having an office and a receptionist made my company more real to me. It did not make it more real to the public. I did a little advertising in the papers, modest black-and-white announcements that did no harm but not much good either. If I was lucky — and I wasn't always — the ad paid for itself by bringing in work I wouldn't otherwise have had. Tawny, the plump literature major who arrived promptly every morning at ten, spent most of her time at the receptionist's desk working on her advice-to-the-lovelorn column for the campus newspaper.

Once she said, "Got a letter here from a guy who's in love with his friend and he doesn't know what to do about it."

"He should just tell her," I said. "Either way, the friendship's going down the tubes, for better or for worse, see what I mean?"

"The friend's a guy."

"So what's the difference?" I said without missing a beat. "Down the tubes, probably for worse, but you never know. Life is full of surprises." She had no need to tell me why this was the only time she'd ever sought my input.

Those early months were not kind to the company account. I came close to letting Tawny go but she beat me to it by quitting. Her campus-newspaper column had led to a more lucrative sex-advice column — *Horny Tawny's Bag of Tricks* — for one of the city's cultural weeklies. From Dickens to dicks — it may not have been as big a leap as it seemed to me at the time.

After I had handed over her last paycheque, she said, "Hey, can I give you a little friendly advice?"

I was wary. Would the advice have anything to do with restraints or leather, unusual uses for ordinary objects or libidinous positions meant only for contortionists?

"Look, I know it's not in your nature — you are the way you are, you know? — but you gotta be more aggressive if you want your business to succeed. They get more calls in an hour at a hot-dog stand than you get here in a week. You ever thought about having some glossy brochures done up with pictures of your work? Ever thought about having a reception for some of your old clients — an opening bash, say, even if it's a little late, but they don't have to know that. Feed 'em a little, water 'em a lot, get 'em talking. Make sure they know you're here. Advertise in the alternative press. There's thousands of professionals out there just dying to support business people from, you know, from their own community. Get with it, man, or you might as well kiss this whole baby of yours goodbye." She slid the folded cheque into her bra, gave me a wink and called "See ya!" over her shoulder as she walked out the door.

I knew immediately that she was right.

Within a week, the ads had been placed. Within two, the brochures had been designed, printed up and distributed. Within three, Ian and Manuel, thrilled that their condo held centre stage in the brochure, had brought along a group of friends to a catered reception that attracted a dozen or so of my former clients plus assorted hangers-on. That evening alone I made six appointments and received an invitation to bid on the design contract for a new upscale restaurant.

Not long after, Tawny's weekly called. They were planning a series of features on young entrepreneurs. What Tawny had told them about me I don't know, but the musical-voiced young man on the phone said I'd been chosen, wasn't that great?

In the page-length article that appeared two weeks later, and which included glowing testimonials from satisfied clients, there was a large photo of me wearing a spacious cotton shirt on loan from a local designer. The photographer had posed me sprawled on a chaise longue. With my slightly hooded gaze staring into the lens and the recently acquired earring glinting from my still-sore right lobe, I looked positively willowy.

THE ARTICLE IS yellowed now in its simple black metal frame but my fondness for it has never waned. I keep it on my office wall along with all the other framed pieces about me that have come along over the years. There I am smiling from the Lifestyle sections of local and national newspapers, from the inside pages of newsmagazines, the covers of decorating magazines, posing at social functions with politicians and their wives, bank presidents and their wives, a film director and his mistress, visiting actors and actresses. There I am in a tuxedo with the bow tie askew, accepting a flute of champagne from a famous author. There I am more casually attired while the prime minister serves me a hamburger from the barbecue set up on the grounds of his official residence. In a drawer somewhere, stacks of audio and videotapes hold the radio and television advertisements from over the years, as well as the interviews I've given about my profession and myself.

It all sounds like celebrity, I know. But it is celebrity of a narrow kind, like that of a gifted surgeon, say, or a brilliant physicist. The circles of recognition are small, the achievements better known than the faces. I can walk down the street and no one would bat an eyelid.

Truth be told, it's not my personality that gets me invited to hobnob. The bank presidents? The coddling of important clients. The famous author? Fundraising for literacy. The movie people? Investment-raising for a film. The prime minister? Donation-raising for an election. Solicitation for AIDS hospices, cancer research, heart research, homeless housing, food-bank funding — the rich man's panhandling, all the rituals of social hypocrisy that grease society's wheels, get me invited everywhere. Should my business ever go under, so would my social life. But I have no fear of that. I am a prudent money manager. My company can weather all but the most devastating of storms.

I've redone the office — no more photos cut from magazines, a colour scheme somewhat bolder than the hackneyed sunset — and have taken over the entire floor to accommodate my staff of four junior designers and various support personnel. Three years ago I bought myself a modest red-brick house, cash, a few kilometres to the east. It's tucked into a leafy cul-de-sac near the ravine and is a long walk or a short bus ride away. It's not without charm, the house, especially when compared with the one I grew up in. But what particularly appealed to me, apart from its location, was the unusually spacious garage tacked onto the side. Finally, I could complete a conversation with my father which had ended in fury many years before. Now I could say, *I have the money, Dad, and I have the garage too.*

ONLY ONCE HAVE I endangered the life I have created for myself. Her name was Caroline and she was a real estate agent. She was on the short side but with a compact body that made her look physically strong. She held herself with confidence. Her hair was short and dark, with little curls falling onto her forehead. Her dark eyes came alive when she smiled, a fan of crow's feet gathering in the corners. One of her front teeth was slightly crooked, a slight imperfection that softened her. She was a very self-possessed woman — at least, that was the impression she gave but I suspect it was partly a construction. I sensed from the very first that she was neither as confident nor as self-possessed as she appeared. It was something she had to work at.

We met one Saturday afternoon when I went to visit potential clients, a couple who'd bought a house that needed redoing from top to bottom. She was with them in the echoing living room when I arrived. I grew agitated the moment I saw her: those dark eyes flickering impatiently towards me then pausing in a long stare that took only a couple of seconds, her entire being radiating an energy that penetrated me like an electrical field. As we toured the house, all four of us, I struggled to see the work I was being shown. Her energy was disrupting my concentration, drawing my attention to her so insistently — to the shape of her ears, the arcs of her brows, the swell of her breasts through her form-fitting blue sweater, her black slacks and sensible leather shoes — that I was numb to everything else. In her presence I felt fully aroused, my mind sharp with the cutting clarity of an early fall morning, every nerve alert to every nuance.

The job went to someone else but I was weeks putting Caroline out of my mind, or at the very least pushing her to the margins.

Then, quite out of the blue one morning, she stopped by the office, ostensibly to pick up information for a client. My blood raced when I saw her — that incredible surge of energy! — and I had to reign in my urge to reach out for her, to get as close as I could to the source of that intense force. I gave her brochures and offered her a coffee. We sat in my office, chatting.

I'd regained my composure, helped probably by being in my own environment, but once we'd finished talking business she seemed to grow nervous, chattering on about an upcoming vacation in the Dominican Republic, about the unpredictability of her work hours, about her brother and his wife who'd just had their first baby.

I only half-heard what she said: my concentration had again softened in the glow she emanated, in her glittery eyes, animated lips, in that slightly crooked front tooth. I could have listened to her talk about the inconsequential for hours on end.

Then she said, "Oh, here I am babbling away, taking up your valuable time." Clutching the brochures in one hand and her purse in the other, she thanked me for the coffee and hurried out.

I shut the door and sat quiet for a few moments, while the office slowly filled again with the air that seemed to have drained away, taking my breath with it.

The next day, to my delight, I received an email from her thanking me for the information and apologizing again for having wasted my time. I sent back an innocuous reply, having deleted from the bottom of my message an invitation to get together for a drink. I'd stared long and hard at that sentence, in the way that I imagine an alcoholic stares at a bottle of gin. Like a lucky addict, I managed to convince myself it was poison.

A few months later, I received a Christmas card from her, a company card, along with her business card with her photo on it, a professional black-and-white shot in half-profile. There was the lick of hair on her forehead, there the dark eyes, there the strong, smiling lips, there — even there! — the riveting energy ...

I sat at the computer and typed out a message:

Dear Caroline, thanks for the card. A Merry Christmas to you too. I want to tell you something. I think a lot about you, about that strange energy you give off, even in this professional black-and-white photo. And just because I think you should know, I admit that my thoughts aren't all, shall we say, innocent and pure. There it is. I needed to tell you. Do what you want with it but I hope you'll take it as the compliment it's meant to be.

Before I could change my mind, I clicked *Send*. Then I sat back in my chair, appalled at what I'd done and thrilled that I'd done it.

HER REPLY WAS waiting for me the next morning:

What am I to do with you? Here you come, complicating my life. Did you act too impulsively? What do you expect of me? Do you want me to walk through a door that swung open the first time we met but that I don't have a key for? A door that swings wide open every time I drive past your office? A door that leads where? I don't know. What do you expect me to tell you? That I think a lot about you too? That sometimes I go out of my way to walk past your office, just trying to give chance a helping hand without quite knowing what I'm expecting? That sometimes I find myself talking to you as if you could hear me? That I was stupefied by the energy circulating around when

NEIL BISSOONDATH

we were in your office drinking that awful coffee? That I recently told a friend that, even though I've only seen you a couple of times, you're one of the few people I would like to see. People say you're gay. I don't believe it, I just think you're a gentle man, and now I have the proof. People also say you're married to your job. I don't know. Look, if I continue like this I'll be able to sell a script to some Hollywood cliché pusher. I don't know what to say. You choose.

I chose. It wasn't hard. I know myself well enough. I've always had several possible ways of being inside of me, none of them fully formed, each offering a life radically different from the others. The one I chose seemed the most promising, the most enticing, in that it offered a life different from my parents'. There was a time when I could still have changed course, but life has a way of diminishing that possibility: the bed you've made becomes the one you're most comfortable in. Only eccentrics who relish their eccentricity, or those whose bed has grown unbearable, would dare make the radical leap from one to another.

I expect nothing of you, Caroline. The facts are what they are. I am married to my job and there's really no place in it for someone else, no matter how tempting. I think I sent you that email because I needed to force myself to confront what I was feeling, to clarify what I want. Now I know. I made my choice a long time ago. My life is made

and I'm happy with it. You're still looking to make yours.
I wish you all the happiness you want.

Her final email said:

Don't you think I know all that? It's okay. I don't want
to make you do anything you don't want to do.

The truth is, had Caroline suggested a roll in the hay, I
would have happily gone along for the ride. But her email
made it clear she was looking for something far more
serious. Still, I liked her so I sent one final line:

The man who seduces you for life will truly be a happy
man.

SO ENDED OUR brief and hesitant dance. I never heard from
her again. To my occasional regret. For a time I found
myself checking the sidewalks from my office window
before leaving, just in case it would be better for me to
exit by the back door. But, truth be told, it wasn't her that
I didn't trust.

All in all, I lived a fairly secluded life, and still do —
one dedicated to promoting my company and protecting
my image. After Caroline, I felt no pressing need for close
companionship and, on occasion, purchased physical
intimacy through an agency specializing in such services.
These encounters always occurred at some medium-

priced downtown hotel, the kind of place that caters to travelling sales reps and bus tours. They were entirely satisfactory. Only once did the lady — and it was always a different lady, variety being life's best spice — think me familiar but, since she'd never been to Akron and this was Bud's first trip here, she dismissed the thought.

This was all I needed. Some rented bodily warmth, the pliancy of purchased flesh to savour for a few delicious moments. Anything else would have been superfluous.

CONSIDERING MY CLIENT base, it's hardly surprising that once in a while an unusual request came my way — unusual for me, that is. One guy who'd recently broken up with his wife — so recently that his ring finger still carried the mark of his absent wedding ring — asked me to turn the unfinished basement of his recently acquired house into a party room. He was juggling with two themes, the Arabian Nights or Alcatraz. I convinced him that steel bars wouldn't do much for the ambiance, and spun images of intimate lighting, Persian rugs, diaphanous curtains, sofas, loads of cushions.

"And mirrors," he said, hiking his pants higher onto his Santa Claus belly. "I want big mirrors, one on each wall." Then he pointed to the far end of the basement where the light from the exposed bulb turned dusky. "And that's where the wall will go."

"The wall?"

"Yeah, the wall. What's a party room without a wall? You know."

But I didn't. And he explained. The wall was to be six feet high and two inches thick; it was to be placed parallel to the far basement wall and about six feet from it. He wanted it covered in camel-coloured felt, with a series of holes cut into it. "About yea high," he said, indicating his crotch. "This big," he added, making a circle by joining the tips of his thumbs and middle fingers.

"How many holes?" I said, scribbling notes as the use of the wall came clear.

"Six should be enough. Some kneeling stools would be nice, eh? One each?"

I told him I knew of a church where I could get some nice ones at a fair price.

He beamed, eyes glittery, wrinkles cording his forehead and flabby cheeks. Shaving his head hadn't shaved the years from his age.

When the work was done some weeks later, he invited me to his first party the following Saturday evening. I declined, pleading a previous engagement.

Through his disappointment, he said, "Well then, maybe we can try out the wall? Won't take long." His voice was shaky. Perspiration beaded above his upper lip.

"Thanks," I said, "But I'm sure it works just fine. Besides, I never mix business with pleasure. Too complicated."

He slipped a cheque from his back pocket, handed it to me. "It's all there in full. Business is over."

I could practically smell his need. There was something pathetic about him, about his middle-aged desperation.

I pocketed the cheque and abandoned him there in the middle of his party room, a sad man made ridiculous by trying too late to be true to himself.

MINE MAY NOT have the appearance of a happy life but it's the life I've chosen, one that leaves me fulfilled and, yes, on the whole happy — certainly happier than my parents ever were. They were like people without choice, my parents: my father labouring for years at a mind-numbing job, my mother going on day after day cooking, cleaning, drinking coffee with her friends in the morning and watching the soaps in the afternoon. I say they were like people without choice because theirs were lives no one would have chosen. *Hey kid, what do you wanna be when you grow up?* I cannot say, and wonder if they would have said, that they were on the whole happy.

One of the ways I relax is by renting a car once in a while and spending a weekend driving around in the country, stopping in at antique shops or at farms with hand-painted signs that promised antiques. The items — everything from rusted ploughs to tarnished candelabra to hand-worked furniture to discarded church pews — are usually battered and grimy and therefore far cheaper than in the city. Bought for a song and restored, these chairs and tables and headboards, unique in their way, can then be resold to clients for a symphony. I often turn these weekends into mini-vacations by spending the night at some comfortable inn or bed-and-breakfast, where people are usually happy to direct you to some likely source of new treasures.

I relish those weekends. They are the only carefree moments I allow myself, which probably explains why they are also the only times that I would enjoy having someone at my side — in the car, at the dining table and, yes, in my bed. Thoughts of Caroline. A sweet ache. But hardly a compelling one.

One early fall weekend, tired after a busy summer, I drove north, away from the city. The air was fresh, it no longer had that singed smell, and the sky was already acquiring hints of that crystalline clarity that intensifies as the weeks go by and the trees drop their foliage. The leaves hadn't yet begun to turn, but the sharp sunshine revealed their exhaustion, their colour thinned to a dusty green.

Stops at several antique shops had proved fruitless. After a simple lunch of salad and two glasses of red wine in a small town now abandoned by the summer hordes — the adjoining lake deserted save for a few solitary fishermen, cottages battened down for winter — I branched off the highway onto a secondary road that would take me past fenced-off fields and farmhouses and, by day's end, to the inn where I'd booked a room for the night. At one point, a herd of young horses raced alongside me until brought up short by the wooden railings that defined their territory, manes flaring as their heads wrenched upwards in disappointment that the game was already over.

At a bend in the road, just past a stand of poplars, a large hand-painted sign promised antiques, a red arrow pointing the way to a barn and farmhouse. I pulled off onto the gravelled driveway and parked beside the barn, next to a rusting tractor. As I got out, a man wearing an untucked red shirt and baggy jeans emerged from the darkness of the barn. "Antiques?" he said, tugging on the visor of his cap in greeting.

"Thought I'd take a look."

"End of season," he said. "Not much left, I'm afraid." Behind him, a golden lab sat on its haunches and gave me a friendly stare.

"That seems to be the story everywhere."

"Better in early summer, after the spring cleaning's done."

It was cool in the barn and my eyes were a few seconds adjusting to the fractured light. "There's the stuff," he said, his hand gesturing me towards a cluttered corner. "Take your time. See anything you like, just give me a holler." He whistled to the dog and together they ambled off towards the rear.

A quick survey told me that he'd spoken the truth. There wasn't much left, not of interest at any rate. Some furniture, a few school desks, a stack of mouldy encyclopedias, an array of rusting farm tools, an incomplete set of silver-plated cutlery, a few brass floor lamps, a confessional, a lectern, wooden cartwheels, boxes of old licence plates — the kind of odds and ends that took a wrong turn at the dump and ended up labelled antiques.

And then, at the very back, behind a stack of dilapidated trunks, I saw a chrome radiator and bullfrog headlights peeping out from under a canvas cover. I tossed back the sheet and my heart raced: a Chevrolet Sedan, four-door, 1928 or '29, six cylinders if I remembered right. The body appeared to be in good condition for a car of its age, no rust that I could see except for a light dusting on the chrome, a few dents, the dull green paint recalling the autumn leaves outside. The fabric of the seats was worn and faded, but under the hood, although I was no mechanic, the motor appeared surprisingly clean. I thought, *To make something old new again.*

"Hey, sir?" I called. "Mister?"

From deeper in the barn came a bark and the sounds of shuffling. The dog trotted in, his tail wagging, followed by the man with a shovel in his hand.

With my palm resting on the radiator, I said, "Is it a kit?"

"Nope, it's the real thing. Belonged to my grandpa."

"How long has it been here?"

"Years and years. Long as I can remember."

"Does it work?"

"You got me there."

"How much?"

He made a face, snatched off his cap and scratched at his greying hair.

A minute later, the Sedan was mine for a song and a half, delivery included.

Part Two

*The body is the servant of the imagination. What takes root
in the mind manifests itself in the flesh.*

She'd come across the words somewhere, perhaps in
one of the yoga books she'd read during her final year at
the university, and they had become for her a truth that
went beyond all others: some things, the words seemed to
suggest, were beyond excuse or justification; they took
root, grew, became part of you.

In the darkness under her eyelids, the body hovering
above hers is without weight, but there is warmth, there
is vigour, there is breath steadily inhaled and exhaled. His
hands cup her breasts with confidence, his thumb and
forefinger — no, his lips, yes, his lips, with their pleasing
connotation of wetness — his lips suck at her nipples,
tugging firmly at the tension he has brought to them.

Between her slightly parted legs, her hand directs his hardness, circling the smooth head around the lips, down one, up the other, pausing to tease that sensitive spot for a second or two before sliding directly down and inserting it into herself, an inch or two, no more, into that warm, moist, tingling aperture, before sliding it back up to — no, not yet, she wants to play some more — his teeth nibbling at her nipple, the pain still this side of pleasurable, the head playing on the surface of the cleft, teasing, promising entry, pressing in a little ...

There is a knock at her bedroom door.

Shit.

"Yes?" She hopes she does not sound breathless. She switches off the vibrator and although its buzz is no louder than a mosquito's — no louder than the electric razor she uses on her legs — the sudden silence seems immense.

"Sumintra," her mother says. "Are you almost ready?"

"I'm shaving my legs, Ma, do you mind?" With a flick of her wrist, she flips the folds of the dressing gown over her bare body. Her hair, still wet from the shower, is wrapped in a towel.

"Again? Didn't you shave just two days ago? I told you electric is not as good as razor but do you listen? Now here you are, wasting time, making your father late."

She glances at the clock radio on the night table. "Ma, it's only nine thirty." The glow through the floor-length sheers promises a sunny day and she wonders whether the perspiration breaking out on her neck and under her arms is from the building summer humidity or her body's reaction to having been denied the crest so easily within reach. On the desk beside the window, her laptop, a birthday gift from her parents, shows the screen saver put in by the dealer in Little India, a photo of the Taj Mahal at sunset, the colours so garish she suspects they were amateurishly enhanced.

"You have to leave earlier today. Don't you remember? You have to go to Lambton. It's a long drive and you know Papu likes to take his time. And there's still the van to pack."

She sits up on the bed and slips the six-inch tube of tapered white plastic into its maroon felt bag. She pulls the drawstring tight. "Fine, fine, let me dry my hair. I'll be there in a minute." As she swings her feet off the bed, she feels the dampness cooling between her legs.

HER FATHER IS stocking the food van in the driveway, methodically dipping into the box cradled on her mother's forearms, picking up the cellophane-wrapped sandwiches and placing them on the refrigerated shelves behind little plastic doors: egg salad, tuna, chicken, ham, cheese, ham and cheese. Despite repeated requests, he will not carry roast beef. A line of perspiration marks his spine through his white cotton shirt and his forehead glistens,

his skin the colour of moist earth. Her mother, greying
hair pulled tight on her scalp and knotted at the back,
glances unhappily at her: she has her own work to do in
the house and she is not pleased to be covering for a
tardy daughter. On the ground beside her are other boxes
with apples, oranges, bananas, salted peanuts, chocolate
bars, muffins, small bags of chips. They haven't brought
out the cooler in which cans of soft drink sit on a bed of
crushed ice, deep within which, well-hidden from prying
eyes, are half a dozen cans of beer for special customers.
When she offers to fetch it from the kitchen, her mother
says, "Get the coffee urn too, and the Styrofoam cups from
the pantry."

She makes three trips between the kitchen and the
van, the large cooler thumping against her thighs, the
cylindrical coffee urn with its spout like a little boy's penis
clutched to her chest, and finally, perspiring heavily now
in her T-shirt and jeans, the bag of disposable cups
dangling as light as a balloon in her hand.

Her father, after quickly ensuring that all is secure, closes
the side panel and latches it shut. Glancing at his watch —
a chunk of stainless steel that keeps him apprised of the
date and time both here and in Calcutta — he says, "It's
time we were going. If we get there early, we can get a
choice spot, hopefully far enough away from the hot-dog-
and-hamburger-man that I won't have to smell his noxious
fumes." He makes the face he always makes when he

thinks of the hot-dog-and-hamburger-man, an expression of disgust that leaves no room for compromise. Sumintra has never told him that she likes hot dogs and hamburgers smothered in ketchup and mustard; it would be enough to send him into cardiac arrest.

Sumintra adjusts her seat belt while her father does the same. Her mother says, "Drive slowly and remember to look out for the trucks." She waves them goodbye and goes into the house. On the seat between them is the metal cash box with a separate compartment for coins of different denominations. From the rear-view mirror dangles a serrated triangle, its pine scent long exhausted. Below it, glued to the dashboard, a miniature plastic Krishna glows in the sunlight.

Two blocks away, as he brakes at the red light before the exit to the highway, her father takes a pack of cigarettes and a lighter from the glove compartment and hands them to her. She eases a cigarette from the pack, lights it and, holding it between thumb and forefinger, passes it to him. Her mother doesn't know he smokes. She would not abide it. The cigarettes are a secret he shares with Sumintra, his only vice — his way of assuaging the pain that comes from being a civil engineer whose qualifications proved so useless on his arrival in this country that he has had to support his family by selling food from a van. Better tobacco, he says, than alcohol. Sumintra, who knows what alcohol has done to her grandfather and her uncle, keeps his secret.

They drive in silence for a while, her father blowing his smoke out the half-opened window. Traffic is light on the highway this Saturday morning and eventually he relaxes behind the wheel. He says, "So, you start work on Monday bright and early for your friend's company."

"Bright and early." One week of drudge work in the accounting department of an architectural firm, but it's well-paid, Kelly has seen to that.

"She is doing well, your friend."

Sumintra sighs, decides it's too beautiful a morning to see his comment as criticism of her. "She designs shopping malls, not exactly what she had in mind at university, but I guess it pays the bills."

In the sky ahead, a jet descends towards the airport. A large transport truck hurtles past them, causing their van to wobble. She sees her father's fingers tighten on the wheel. He has a particular fear of trucks ever since seeing one lose control in front of him and, in a thunderous crash, reduce a small car to scrap metal. He had stopped and, with others, had tried to help the occupants of the car but there was nothing to be done. "Bits and pieces," he had said. "Just bits and pieces."

"Kelly," he says, his eyes still on the ever-diminishing truck. "It is a funny name for a girl."

"Her name's Kelly-Ann." She knows what he's getting at. Boys with names like John or David or Andy — or Kelly — are threats. Unlike boys with names like Ranjit or Ashok or Yogendra, they are the very prospect of annihilation. Like the roundness of the earth or the purity of the Ganges or the holiness of Krishna, it is a subject never to be raised, a notion never to be challenged.

"You must invite her home for dinner one day. Does she enjoy Indian cooking?"

"Never asked her."

He's never suggested this before, although she's known Kelly for almost four years. The idea doesn't appeal to her in the least. The conversation would surely veer towards Kelly's work, their friendship at university, and her mother would probably remark, shaking her head in that sorrowful way that suggests an immutable pain, how it was too bad that Sumintra had chosen to leave architecture — already bad enough: no doctor or biologist or geneticist for them — for English literature and wasn't it wonderful that Kelly had stuck with it and was doing so well.

But Kelly is part of one world, her parents are part of another. Sumintra, who moves with ease between them, has no desire to invite one into the other.

Her father, glancing into the rear-view mirror, says, "I have to stop at the Kumars. It'll only take a minute."

"Why the Kumars?"

"I have a little temple business to discuss with Arjun."

The Kumars are people she does not like, people of standing in her parents' community. Mr. Kumar, whose import company is one of the biggest suppliers of saris

and dhotis and religious paraphernalia in Canada, holds a
position of prominence at the temple they attend twice
a week and from which they return home smelling of smoke
and burnt ghee. People come to him looking for favours.
He is a big man, and loud, with lips that appear to be constantly wet. No one is more impressed with him than he is
with himself. As for his wife, Sumintra has often thought
her the prototype for the scheming shrew that inhabits the
Bollywood movies her parents sometimes rent — the one
with too much jewellery, a precarious smile and plans for
everyone else's life.

Sumintra says, "Their son — what's his name?"

"Mohan."

"Yes, Mohan. He wouldn't happen to be home from
grad school, would he?"

"Why, as it happens, Mohan is spending a few days with
his parents before going off to a summer job with Microsoft
in Seattle. Arjun was telling me recently that he will be
getting his MBA in the fall and that the position just might
be made permanent. At least, so he is hoping."

Once, when she was a teenager, her parents had dragged
her along to the temple for the Diwali celebrations. Mohan
had been pointed out to her as the son of the big man.
She remembers a plump, moon-faced boy full of self-
importance at being the son of the father, his manner among
the children the same as his father's among the adults.

"Papu, we wouldn't be stopping in at the Kumars just

THE SOUL OF ALL GREAT DESIGNS

because he's there, would we?"

"Why, daughter, what are you accusing me of?"

"You know what I'm accusing you of."

He laughs. "Hypothetically, if Mohan were to ask you out, what would you say?"

"Hypothetically, it would be for him to ask me and for me to answer him."

"So that's not a definite no."

"That's not a definite yes either, Papu."

She thinks it not impossible that the plump boy has grown into a sleek man and that his self-regard has tempered into self-confidence.

THE KUMARS' HOUSE is in a more upscale subdivision than her parents'. This means that if her father spends twenty minutes or so every summer weekend pushing a powerless mower back and forth along their lawn, Mr. Kumar needs to spend an hour or more driving his tractor mower around theirs. It means that, instead of broadcasting grains of fertilizer and herbicide by gloved hand as her father does, Mr. Kumar pays a lawn-care company to nourish the soil and kill off the weeds. It means that the house is higher and wider and longer, that the car in the garage is bigger, newer and more powerful. It means that what is labour for her father is play for Mr. Kumar.

This is what she thinks as they drive through the quiescent neighbourhood, past big, bright houses and a trim, well-appointed children's playground, towards the Kumars' house. Success can be defined not by what you have to do but by what you choose to do.

Mr. Kumar is out front, riding his tractor mower along the edge of the lawn. He is wearing a floppy tennis hat, a white T-shirt that encases his protuberant belly, grey work trousers and white tennis shoes. When their van pulls into the driveway, he looks up and raises his left hand in greeting. The gold watch strapped to his wrist catches the sun.

Her father turns off the engine, pulls up the handbrake. Sumintra says, "Not long?"

He takes the key from the ignition. "Just a few minutes."

"Can I wait for you here?"

"Don't be silly, daughter."

Mr. Kumar dismounts from the green machine that looks like a miniature replica of farm machinery and treads across the lawn towards them. He opens Sumintra's door for her. "Ahh, what a beautiful young lady you have become! How are you, Sumintra?"

She stumbles a little as she gets out of the van. "Just fine, Mr. Kumar. How are you? How's the sari business?"

He leans down to give her a kiss but her hand is faster and, after a second of confusion, she wins. He shakes her hand instead.

Her father comes around the truck. Mr. Kumar claps his large palms down onto her father's shoulders. "Manny, how are things, my friend?"

Manny? She has never heard anyone except a few regular customers, whose Southern-European tongues can't handle Manohar, call her father *Manny*. One more reason for disliking Mr. Kumar. But if her father is offended, he lets nothing show. He nods, he smiles, he displays once again the sunny disposition he's known for.

"Come inside," Mr. Kumar says. "Pinkie's waiting for us. She's prepared a little something."

Alarmed, Sumintra says, "That's very kind but we're kind of in a hurry, we've got to get to —"

"Nonsense, nonsense," Mr. Kumar says, pressing her father toward the house.

Sumintra says, "Papu, Lambton, remember?"

Mr. Kumar takes her by the elbow and tugs her along. "Lambton, it's a nice place, some of our people live there, but it's not going anywhere, it'll still be there later."

Sumintra frowns at her father but, propelled along by Mr. Kumar's large palm, he doesn't see her disapproval.

Mr. Kumar says, "You haven't lived till you've tasted my Pinkie's *dhalpuri*. As light as rice paper and as tasty as, well, as tasty as anything you've ever eaten. She has a way with the spices, my Pinkie. Besides, she's been up since five making them, they couldn't be fresher. You don't want to break her heart, do you?"

Sumintra thinks she wouldn't mind trying — it would be a challenge to put a crack in that stone. But then she thinks that anybody who's had to go through life known as Pinkie has probably suffered enough humiliation and she resigns herself to tasting Pinkie's *dhalpuris*.

After the brightness outside, the light inside the house is lustreless, sombre, and the scent of fresh-cut grass gives way to a whiff of disinfectant. They remove their shoes and place them on a rubber mat set beside the door for that purpose.

Mr. Kumar snatches off his cap and crumples it into a ball in his palm. "Pinkie," he shouts, his voice echoing into the depths of the house. "Manny and Sumintra are here."

The slap of leather slippers on the parquet floor is followed by Mrs. Kumar's pebbly voice calling out, "Welcome! Welcome!" which is followed by Mrs. Kumar herself. She is a tall woman whose suspiciously black hair sits nested on the crown of her head and whose bottle-green sari is wound as tight as plastic wrap on her stringy body. Jabbing her gold-framed glasses higher on her nose, she presses her palms together and bows her head slightly in greeting. "Manny, you look well."

Her father returns the greeting. "And you appear to be in the pink of health, if I may say so, Mrs. Kumar."

Mrs. Kumar? Does her father — *Manny* to them both — call Mr. Kumar *Mr. Kumar*, too?

"And Sumintra." Mrs. Kumar's assessing eyes turn towards her: the inspection, the summing up, takes about a second. "A little girl just yesterday and now look at you. What a lovely young woman you have become. Such thick hair, such light skin. You must have suitors lined up at your door."

"Dozens and dozens," Sumintra says, and she enjoys the disapproval that flashes furtively in Mrs. Kumar's eyes.

Her father gives an uncomfortable chuckle that is like a warning to her. "You have redecorated since my last visit," he says. "The walls were blue, if I'm not mistaken. This pink is much more becoming, it is very nice. You chose it?"

"A good thing too," Mr. Kumar says, evidently pleased by the compliment to his wife. "If it had been me, we would be looking at mustard walls or saffron walls, or fire brigade red. My wife understands that the eyes need restful colours at the end of a hard day."

Mrs. Kumar gives him a grateful smile and excuses herself: the snacks are just about ready.

At Mr. Kumar's invitation, Sumintra perches on the edge of the sofa beside her father while he drops into an armchair across from them and launches into a long lamentation about the untrustworthiness of the workers in the factories back home, a growing restiveness among them that is leading to growing shoddiness, which the factory owners must quash with a heavy hand or risk losing the large orders he places every year. His complaints unfurl like an endless bolt of cloth, sentences separated by commas with no periods in sight. Her father, seemingly unaware of the passing time, nods in wordless sympathy. Sumintra has an inkling of the working conditions in those factories, but she has already been warned once.

The Kumars' living room seems strangely at odds with the house. Heavy drapes at the windows deny the sunshine outside and the glow that survives the passage is absorbed by furniture that is dark and heavy, Old World. The armchairs and sofa, of stolid, polished wood, are upholstered in a rough fabric dizzy with swirling patterns of gold and green, like mustard stirred into moss. In the middle of the room, a circular brass table with a variety of brass gods drawn up in military formation sits on a spindly-legged trestle, which sits on a blood-red rug, which sits on the shiny, blond parquet floor. In one corner, a teak chest holds a clutter of framed photographs, some colour, most black and white. The walls are bare but for a series of amateurish paintings, the Taj Mahal, some kind of mud-hut village, a brown smudge that might be the Ganges. A sliding door at the far end of the living room is obscured by a wooden folding-screen perforated by dozens of holes, each a splatter of light.

Sumintra thinks that if the house, large and modern as it is, suggests a certain lightness, the decor is like heavy ballast weighing it down. She wonders how the Kumars can breathe indoors.

Mr. Kumar, his disquisition exhausted, takes a deep breath. "You know, Manny," he says, "this is my favourite part of the weekend, besides the puja, of course. I spend so much time in my office, negotiating and cajoling and buying and selling, dealing with incompetent salesmen and lazy customs people and checking inventory and shipping orders — it is not good for the health. To be outside, in nature, smelling the air, smelling the grass, feeling the sun ... I envy you, Manny, your job means that you are outside all the time, you are a lucky man."

"I know, Arjun. Not a day goes by that I do not thank God for my luck."

Luck? Sumintra thinks. Does Mr. Kumar know how her father earns his living? Has he ever seen him returning home at the end of a long day of driving from construction site to construction site, getting out the cash box and checking the day's take and, as often as not, sighing away his disappointment? Has he ever heard her father's neck crackling away the day's tensions, his glazed eyes staring into the mid-distance at hopes growing dimmer still? You asshole, she thinks, you stupid, fucking asshole. The words begin shaping themselves on her tongue and she nibbles at her lower lip until it hurts. "I've got an idea," she says brightly. "Why don't you two switch jobs? It would be —"

But Mrs. Kumar saves her by trundling a wooden tea cart into the living room. On it are a platter of rolled *dhalpuri*, a jar of orange juice surrounded by four clear-plastic cups and a small stack of plastic dessert plates with paper napkins.

Mr. Kumar claps his palms together. "Ahh, here come the refreshments."

Her father takes advantage of the distraction to give her a little nudge and a warning glance. She replies with a flicker of her lower lip.

At Mrs. Kumar's insistence, they all lean forward to help themselves.

Mr. Kumar, chewing, says, "Pinkie, where is the boy? He should come pay his respects to our visitors."

Sumintra thinks: No. It is the moment she has been dreading.

"He is in his bedroom," she says. "Studying, studying, it is all he does." Her gaze shifts to Sumintra. "He is going to work for Microsoft in Seattle." Then it shifts to her father. "He is a very hard worker, our Mohan."

Mr. Kumar says, "Go tell him to take a break and come say hello."

Mrs. Kumar puts down the pitcher of juice and hurries off, her sandals flapping on the floor.

Sumintra thinks that perhaps the years have transformed him. After all, she was no head-turner back then.

Mr. Kumar, taking another bite of *dhalpuri*, says, "Like father, like son. He works too hard. All that time shut up alone in his room is not good for the health."

Sumintra wonders briefly about all that time Mohan spends shut up alone in his room: just studying or practising his equivalent of her shaving her legs? She pushes away the image of the plump teenager she once met, stretched out on his bed, eyes closed, doing the ol' cock-a-doodle-doo as Kelly puts it.

Mr. Kumar, moving with the weary ease of a big man, reaches for the pitcher of juice and splashes the plastic cups full. He serves Sumintra, then her father.

The flap of Mrs. Kumar's sandals announces her return. Shuffling along behind her is Mohan and Sumintra sees that the plump boy has grown into a plump man, with the height of his mother and the bulk of his father. His hair is closely cropped. The years have brought him glasses. The thick rectangular lenses and black plastic frame suggest a practical bent that makes no concession to style. The tails of his blue shirt hang outside his trousers and the sleeves are pushed back to his elbows. Below the hem of his khaki cargo pants, his bare feet spill over the edges of his blue flip-flops.

Her father gets to his feet, puts out his hand. "Mohan, it is good to see you. Congratulations on your success. May it grow in leaps and bounds."

Mohan shakes her father's hand. "Thank you, sir. It's good to see you again."

Mr. Kumar, clutching the pitcher in both hands, says, "You remember Sumintra, of course."

Mohan blinks his dark eyes at her. She sees that he has no memory of her — there is no reason he should. He says, "Of course."

Sumintra thinks: Liar. She says, "Hi. I hear you're off to Seattle."

He nods, slides his hands into his pants pockets. "You been there?"

"No. Vancouver was as close as I got. A school trip. High school."

"Ah."

Mr. Kumar hands the pitcher to his wife, turns to her father. "Manny, why don't we go to my study and get business out of the way?"

Her father nods, puts his orange juice down on the tea table and follows Mr. Kumar out of the living room.

Mrs. Kumar says, "Oh, where is my head? I have a cake in the oven."

Sumintra thinks: Here we go.

Urging Mohan to have a piece of *dhalpuri*, Mrs. Kumar bustles away to the kitchen, slippers flapping on the floor like the opening strains of a tedious soundtrack.

Mohan slides his hands from his pockets and throws himself into the armchair vacated by his father. He looks squarely at Sumintra. "Alone at last," he says with a sarcasm that immediately lightens her tension. "Sorry 'bout that. Sometimes my folks can be as subtle as an earthquake."

"An earthquake?"

"I'm going to Seattle, remember? It's kind of on my mind."

She laughs. "They engineered this, didn't they?"

"Gee, think so?"

"They didn't tell you either?"

"Would I look as if I just rolled out of bed if I'd known I was going to meet a prospective bride? Now I know why my mom's been after me all morning to shower and shave. She wanted me to change before coming down."

"My dad suddenly had to see your dad about business."

Mohan shakes his head, a tolerant smile rising on the lips he has inherited from his father.

Sumintra says, "Just so I know — you didn't actually change, did you?"

The smile gives way to a low laugh. "Just so you know — this is my Sunday best."

"Today's Saturday."

"So now you know the sad truth." He leans forward in the armchair, clasps his hands. "They're probably expecting me to ask you out, you know."

"Probably." She remembers her father's hypothetical question, but decides to keep it to herself.

"So what do you think?"

"I don't think so."

"Me neither. Look, I'm sure you're a really nice person and all that, but I'm just not ready for that kind of thing. I'm concentrating on my career right now and for the next few years."

"Me, too. Let's not mention a thing and maybe it'll all go away."

"Fine by me."

She senses in the silence that follows that they have exhausted all they have in common: their desire not to go out with each other. It is time to make conversation but she senses, too, that making small talk is not one of Mohan's strengths. She says, "Look, I know you're busy. Don't let me keep you. I'm happy here. I'll just stuff myself with more of your mother's *dhalpuri*."

"You kidding? My mom would kill me."

In her mind, the plump man with an unexpectedly mellifluous voice and ugly glasses replaces the plump boy playing cock-a-doodle-doo in his bedroom. The image is not unpleasant and she surprises herself by entertaining it for a few seconds. Then she shakes it off and says, "Who did the paintings?"

"Me. Did them on my last trip to India. My mom's convinced I'm a gifted painter." He glances at the paintings. "She's got no taste for art, my mom. I was just killing time."

"You go often?"

"My folks go every couple of years. I join them when I can. It's not easy, with studies and work and all. You been there?"

"Once, when I was little. Don't remember a thing."

"Your parents don't go back?"

"My mom went a few years ago. My dad had to work." The truth is that they couldn't afford two tickets but she doesn't want to say that.

"And you?"

"Summer school."

"Ah."

MR. KUMAR, PADDING across the lawn towards his miniature tractor, waves goodbye to them.

Sumintra, adjusting the seat belt on her shoulder, says,
"You guys are so transparent. As subtle as an earthquake, as
Mohan said."

"What are you talking about, daughter?" He eases the
van onto the exit ramp, the multi-lane highway opening
up before them. The traffic is a little heavier than earlier,
but still manageable.

"You didn't have any business with Mr. Kumar. You just
wanted to get me and Mohan together and watch the
sparks fly, right?"

"Perhaps not sparks," he says, gaze shifting to the rear-
view mirror as he guides the van to the centre lane.
"Maybe just to see if there might be any warmth there, I
admit. But it is true that I had business with Arjun. I was
just killing two birds with one stone."

"Fine, then. Dead birds can't lay eggs."

"You didn't like Mohan?"

"Not my type."

"I didn't know you had a type, daughter."

"Neither did I."

Despite himself — she hears the hesitation in his voice — her father laughs.

From either side of the highway, glass-and-concrete factories gaze down at them. Overhead, an airplane large enough to transport the population of a decent-sized village seems to hover like a suspended condor, its undercarriage deployed for landing.

For Sumintra, this whole question of *type* is a complicated one. She has never been able to define her tastes so precisely that they narrow to a label. Kelly — whom she met in ENV-101: Introduction to Pollution and then followed to FEM-102: From Paragon to Paramour to Pussy, Women's Evolution in Western Civilization — has more than once enumerated the parameters she seeks in a man: tall, handsome, well-built and well-hung, a certain intelligence, a sense of humour and knowing his place. At first Sumintra didn't take her seriously but as she has watched one man after another winding his short path through Kelly's life, she has had to admit that Kelly respects her own declared tastes. The stream of Kevins and Cals and Lances and Bricks has fused in her mind into a single generic being whose gleaming smile, wide shoulders and muscular legs are animated by a kind of vacuous sociability. Sumintra isn't sure that Kelly's parameters have served her well. A man's presence in her life infuses her with a breathless, eager-to-please desperation that has led her to leap out of airplanes, bungee jump from bridges, rappel down cliffs. And Kelly seems no happier for all that.

Sumintra says, "What business did you have with Mr. Kumar?"

"Nothing to worry yourself about," her father says, his face stiffening into the mask which he believes to be neutral and, so, disarming.

"Is it temple business or business business?"

"Just business."

"Come on, Papu, out with it. You're not negotiating a dowry or anything like that, are you?"

"Actually, we are at your body weight in gold and three sheep. They are demanding three goats as well. We think you are worth only one."

"Papu!"

"If you go on a diet it would help on the gold side."

Sumintra's chest grows warm with a ballooning of affection for her father. It's been ages since he's teased her like this. She reaches out, squeezes his arm and is rewarded with a smile and, quickly, a glance from his mischievous eyes. He has never told her that he loves her, but he has never needed to.

Up ahead, a police cruiser with flashing lights provides cover for a stalled car. A tow truck is pulling off onto the verge behind them.

Sumintra says, "I know it's none of my business, Papu, but are you having problems? Everybody knows Mr. Kumar

helps people out. You can tell me, I'm not a kid anymore."
They are out in the country now, rolling past lightly
undulating fields and outcroppings of reddish rock. It's
growing warm in the van.

Her father takes a deep breath. As they drive past the
cruiser, he lets the van slow just a bit even though he's
going ten kilometres per hour below the speed limit. She
knows that for the next minute or so his eyes will flit
constantly to the rear-view mirror to ensure that the cruiser
is not coming in pursuit. Reassured, he sinks deeper into
his seat, hands at ten and two on the steering wheel.
"Business is quite good, daughter. I make more than a pit-
tance. I owe Arjun a little money, that's all."

"Still? I thought you'd paid that off by now." She knows
that when her parents wanted to buy the house ten years
before, cash had been short. Mr. Kumar had made up the
shortfall in the down payment.

"Not the down-payment money, daughter. We paid that
off lickety-split. He's helped us out a few times since."

"You borrowed more money from him?"

"Expenses. You know. Nothing for you to worry about."

"What kind of expenses?" Sumintra feels the rise of a
vague, familiar guilt. In high school, then at university,
while all her friends held part-time jobs — babysitting or
selling clothes or tending the cash register in corner stores
— she sat at home leisurely doing her homework, helping
out a bit in the kitchen and with the vacuum cleaner,

reading, learning to watercolour. Her job, her parents always insisted, was to concentrate on getting good marks at school. Still, there was that haunting sight of her father sitting at the kitchen table counting out the pennies, nickels, dimes and quarters.

He taps the top of the steering wheel with the flat of his hand. "You remember when the transmission gave out? The shingles began peeling from the roof of the house? Then the oil tank had to be replaced and the property taxes paid."

Sumintra is silent for a moment, confronting the list of unsuspected expenses. There is one he hasn't mentioned. "And then there were my school fees," she says.

His eyelids blink rapidly. "And then there were your school fees," he says.

"And my books and my clothes. My spending money."

"Yes."

She wishes he would look at her, but he keeps his narrowed eyes fixed on the undulating road ahead.

"Life is an expensive proposition, daughter. We all start off as under-ducks."

"Under*dogs*, Papu."

"I know that, but a dog is always a dog. Under-ducks, however, may one day, with luck and perseverance, be able to flap their wings and fly with the others, maybe even above them."

She knows this ploy of his — say something clever,

divert the conversation — but she won't play along this time. "You shouldn't have borrowed money to pay for my schooling. I could have helped."

"But you already had a job."

"Stop it, Papu. That's an old story. It doesn't justify borrowing money from Mr. Kumar."

"He is a good man. He lends money to many people in our community. His interest rate is better than the bank's."

Sumintra knows this is an argument she cannot win. Her father would rather incur debt than fail to give her an approximation of his childhood: rigorous schooling, carefree holidays, adult responsibility reserved for adulthood. She remembers telling Kelly about this — already, at university, she worked part-time at the architectural firm that would offer her a permanent job at graduation — and she remembers Kelly's envy. She remembers too how Kelly, after a sip of her wine, put a finger to her chin and said, "But the price you pay is having to live at home." She didn't have to say that it seemed too big a price.

Her father opens the glove compartment, fishes out the cigarettes and the lighter and passes them to her. She lights one, gives it to him, then lights one for herself.

As she rolls down the window, her father says, "I didn't know you smoke, daughter."

"I don't. But it's nice to try something new once in a while, don't you think?"

"It is a good philosophy," he says, smoke streaming from his nostrils.

SHE HAD SMOKED her first joint sitting cross-legged on the unmade bed in Kelly's dorm room, the fluorescent light above the built-in desk growing milky and opaque until it seemed to cascade over the stacks of books and notepads. It was the only time the light behaved this way for the rest of that first semester and her regret was brief when, the following September, Kelly announced that her asthma had caused her to give up grass over the summer.

It was Kelly who, in the summer following their second year, introduced her to cottage country. For a week one summer, she discovered a different way of life two hours north of the city. In her parents' circle, no one owned a cottage. The idea of "going to the cottage" was alien to people whose spare money was either sent back home to relatives or hoarded for plane tickets to the land they had left only physically. So Kelly's family cottage was a revelation, unsettling in that it suggested there was so much she didn't know about other lives and other ways of living.

There were two wooden cottages, both painted white. They sat facing the lake on a large stretch of grassy land. The smaller, more modern one was for the parents, the other, weather-beaten despite the new coat of white paint, closer to the sandy beach, for the children. Each had a mosquito-netted porch out front with cushioned rattan chairs for admiring the sunsets and, later in the evening, for playing cards in irresolute yellow light. At the edge of the lake, which was so large she couldn't see the other side, a collection of watercraft — a rowboat, a canoe, a paddleboat — lay beached and unguarded. Out on the water, speedboats went by, sometimes dragging along skiers.

They were alone at the cottage. The rest of Kelly's family and invited friends came only on weekends and there were few other cottagers around, people whose greetings were friendly enough but which also suggested a wish to be allowed to get on with their holidaying. Sumintra and Kelly spent lazy hours lying in the sun or walking on the beach, swimming in the frigid water. They would prepare simple salads for lunch and more elaborate suppers which they ate in the porch while drinking beer from the bottle and playing Scrabble or checkers.

The beer made Kelly drowsy and she usually went to bed early, leaving Sumintra alone in the living room where she would happily shuffle through the small bookcase in the corner. She flicked through old copies of *Reader's Digest* for the jokes, pushed aside the musty stack of *Archie & Jughead* comics in favour of yellowed albums of *Peanuts*. She speed-read dog-eared Agatha Christies and

Raymond Chandlers but couldn't get on with the Perry Masons. Her professors would have been appalled at her reading material, and the thought itself gave her pleasure after the months spent performing autopsies on novels. In one course evaluation, she had wondered why no professor ever asked if they had liked a book. Was pleasure, she wrote with the courage of anonymity, pointless to the pointy-headed?

On the third night, not long after Kelly went to bed, she was flipping through an issue of *National Geographic* when, through the window, a streak of golden light caught her eye. Her head jerked upwards in a spasm of fear and for a few breathless seconds her head filled with the scream of jet engines, a maelstrom of air buffeting through an airplane cabin angled towards the earth, her mother's cousin — the faces from the photo in her parents' bedroom tightened by wind and terror — hugging her two young daughters to her chest. Through the howl of the raging engines she heard screams. Her body began tilting forward as if it were being drawn irresistibly into the drag of the aircraft.

With an effort of will, she freed herself from the paralysis that had come to her. The magazine rustled from her hands to the floor. She lunged towards the window. Hundreds of golden streaks scored the black sky. Shooting stars. They were only falling stars, curtains of them blazing for a few seconds before winking out. They were not that other Sumintra and her daughters hurtling with three hundred and twenty-six people towards extinction.

THE VAN CRESTS a hill and begins easing down the other side. Her father rubs at his eyes with one hand. "It's going to be a hot one today," he says. "The crowd will be thirsty. I hope we have packed enough cool drinks."

Sumintra wishes she could have a cool drink now to wash away the bitter taste the cigarette has left in her mouth. She licks her lips, gathers saliva on her tongue, swallows it. "Papu."

"Yes, daughter?"

"Tell me again why you named me Sumintra."

"Hah! You know why."

"Tell me again."

He glances into the rear-view mirror, checks his speed. "You know about your mother's cousin."

"Sometimes I feel like I've become a memorial to her, Sumintra Take Two."

"That was not the way it was intended. That was the way it worked out. She was your mother's closest friend. I don't know how she would have made it without Sumintra when we first moved here. Sumintra showed her around, introduced her to people, showed her where to shop for all those things she couldn't find in supermarkets.

Sumintra was there in the delivery room when you were born. You should have seen how her face lit up when we told her we would name our first-born after her. Later she told your mother that only the birth of her twins had ever made her happier." At the mention of the twins, his voice wavers, falls off. He sighs. "Pria and Vashti would probably be married now, with children of their own."

She lets the thought dissipate in its own good time, the steady growl of the van's engine erasing the words and the feeling they had borne.

"Sometimes I feel as if Mamu wants me to live Sumintra's life for her, and maybe the twins' lives, too."

"When has she ever said that, daughter? This is your imagination. Your life is your life, it is nobody else's."

A rocky, undulating landscape unfurls on both sides of the truck, terrain worked and shaped but, even in the sunshine, stark to the point of desolation. A chill creeps up Sumintra's back. She says, "Kelly calls me Sue. Sometimes I think I prefer that name. It's easier to deal with."

"I am sorry your name is a burden to you, daughter." From the hardening in her father's voice, she understands she has gone too far. "The perpetrators may never be punished. It is therefore all the more important that we keep Sumin and the girls alive in our hearts and our minds. Your part in this does not strike me as being terribly onerous."

"So you admit that my life isn't completely my own, then?"

"Nobody's life ever is, Sumintra. As you get older, you will come to understand that we parcel pieces of our life out to others. Not to do so would be to defy God."

Sumintra crosses her arms and stares at her running shoes. When her father starts talking about God, it's time to shut up.

THE BEAUTY OF the burning stars soothed the rawness in her chest, kindled a kind of thrill. She needed to share this moment, the spectacle too much for her alone. Light still glowed under Kelly's door. She pushed the door open.

"Hey, Kel, you've got to come see —"

She froze in the doorway.

Kelly was lying on the narrow bed, her dark-blonde hair splayed on the pillow, her nightgown pulled up to her waist. Her left leg was drawn up, her right hanging over the edge of the mattress. Between her legs, her right hand was grasping what appeared to be a thick black tube. The other end of the tube was inside her. A soft buzzing sound came from it. Sumintra said, "Oh my god." She quickly backed away and pulled the door shut.

She was standing at the window with her stomach knotted, staring out at the star-streaked darkness, when Kelly's door squeaked open. She turned around.

Kelly, barefoot, in her nightgown, tossed her hair back and looked straight at her. "It's not nice to interrupt a girl when she's having fun."

Sumintra threw her hands up. "I'm so sorry, Kel, I should have knocked. I was just so excited by the shooting stars, I wanted you to see them."

Kelly shrugged. "I've seen them dozens of times."

"I hope you're not mad?"

"I'm not mad." She seemed, if anything, a little sad, deflated.

Sumintra glanced out the window. The show was over. Kelly walked over to the sofa and sat, folding her legs under her. Sumintra bent down and picked up the *National Geographic*. Smoothing out the pages, she said, "What was that thing?"

Kelly squinted at her, then snickered. "You know what it was. Don't pretend. Or haven't you ever seen a dildo before?"

Dildo. The word startled Sumintra: it had such an ugly sound. "Not when it was — you know — in use."

"Are you shocked?"

"Not shocked. Just surprised, I guess. Embarrassed."

Kelly said, "I could use a beer right about now. You?" She eased herself off the couch and went to the kitchen.

Sumintra followed and, standing in the white glare from the fridge, waved away a bottle of beer in favour of a bottle of apple juice. The door rattled shut, the kitchen returned to shadow in the refracted light from the living room.

Kelly twisted the cap from the bottle, took a swig. "You know, Sue, sometimes I just need it, when the tension builds up. I mean, it's easy enough to find on campus but sometimes I'm just not in the mood to go out trawling. Out here there's nobody, at least nobody who wouldn't go blabbing about it. So, once in a while, Richard comes to the rescue."

"Richard? You've given it a name?"

"Well, we're on intimate terms. Think of the short form."

Sumintra thought for second. "Oh." She laughed. "You're crazy."

Kelly moved over to the table, drew back a chair, sat. "I'm not crazy. I just recognize my needs, that's all. I mean, don't you ever go crazy sometimes, you just need it so bad?"

Sumintra leaned against the fridge, became aware of its low hum. Her face was burning and she thought she should have taken a beer. "Uh, Kelly, you know, I've never, um, with a guy, I mean."

"You've never ... Ever?" Kelly's eyes widened to white in the gloom.

Sumintra nodded.

"You do like guys, right?"

"Of course I do."

"And you do have feelings, right? I mean, you're not dead down there."

"No, not dead."

"So do you scratch the itch sometimes at least?"

"Sometimes."

Kelly took a swig of the beer. "Man," she said, "when you meet the guy who makes you tingle, you're going to explode!"

Sumintra said, "I think I'll have a beer after all."

At her birthday two months later, Kelly gave her a small box wrapped in paper decorated with exploding stars. Inside, within a felt bag, was a small, tubular vibrator in white plastic. On a card, Kelly had written: *It's about time you met Richard's little brother. Batteries not included.*

Holding it in the tips of her fingers, she placed it on her desk, contemplated it for a long minute. There was something vaguely culinary about it. She could see it lying inoffensive among cooking spoons, cleavers, carving knives, basters. She was relieved it wasn't shaped like the real thing. Its tapered end suggested a tool designed for easy insertion into narrow spaces.

Then she thought of those spaces and hurriedly slipped the vibrator back into its bag, plopped the bag back into its box and buried the box at the bottom of a drawer chaotic with pens and pencils and rulers and chains of paper clips. If her mother ever came across it, she would assume it was some kind of drafting pen.

FOLLOWING THE CONTOURS of the land, the road straightens out, the fields to either side displaying a green stubble. Her father lets the van slow as a large convertible speeds by on their left. It is a long, wide car painted red, its tail — with small fins and oval brake lights and a chrome bumper — vaguely reminiscent of drawings of fantasy space vehicles she saw in a magazine at Kelly's cottage. Although the car looks heavy and sits low to the ground, Sumintra imagines it peeling from the earth and climbing, with a steep bank to the left, into the blue sky.

Her father says, "We will be there soon. That is Mr. French's '59 Pontiac Parisienne convertible. He loves that car more than he loves his wife. In fact, that is the third Mrs. French in the passenger seat. If I am not mistaken, Mr. and Mrs. Greene will be at the show too with their '65 Chevrolet Impala. I do believe that Mrs. Greene might one day become the fourth Mrs. French."

"Too bad for Mr. Greene."

"Oh no, daughter. Mr. Greene, I believe, already has his eye on Mrs. Nash. She is a divorcee, you know. She got the '68 Mustang GT convertible in the divorce settlement. Mr. Greene prefers the sporty type."

"What's happened to Mr. Nash?"

"A sad story. After divorce, he bought a Hyundai." He glances at her. When their eyes meet, they both laugh.

Sumintra is always surprised at the detailed information her father gleans from the classic cars and their owners.

Over three years of selling refreshments at their summer gatherings, he has grown conversant in their language. He knows the cars by manufacturer, by model, by cylinder. He knows about the hammers and the spanners and the screwdrivers they use, the welding torches and the buffers. He knows that breathing masks and earmuffs and goggles are vital and that hats are recommended for protecting hair from soot. He knows what a hundred-point restoration is, and a frame-up, and how many hours of work can be spent in giving new life to old things. He knows that some of the owners love the smell of rust and hot metal and burning rubber, while others will work only on rust-free cars, and still others will buy a car only when it has been completely restored by someone else.

He knows the origins of their passions: their father's first car, their first car, the car of teenaged dreams too rich for teenaged pockets, the car that evokes a world which now seems fresh and innocent and full of promise. He knows how that passion can balloon, so that one couple redecorated their house in the style of a '60s diner to match their '66 Rambler American.

And he knows of those — they are his favourites — who will talk of finding what one man called orphan cars, cars long abandoned, given up for lost, and resurrect them with an attention to detail that requires intricate and painstaking research. It is not the finished product that motivates them; it is the care they lavish on the project, the refusal to compromise, the endless searches for an original part, an original seat fabric, an original colour. They are people who believe that nothing ever truly disappears and that everything can be rescued and given a new future. He has said they are the most optimistic people he's ever met.

When her father talks about this world of classic cars, one he fell into through selling snacks and sandwiches and cold drinks, he seems the least like himself — at least, the self she has always known. He says, and she believes him, that he has no desire to be the owner of a classic car, no desire to put in the expense and the labour and to gather with others on summer weekends. He is simply fascinated by a world so different from his own, perhaps not aware of how that flirtation changes him.

On the roadway ahead of them now, evidence of the gathering: her father identifies for her Mr. Corbett's yellow Ford A Roadster, Mr. Marvin's '56 Hudson, Mr. Kennedy's '39 Cadillac, each shining like a jewel in the sun. Then he tells her about Mr. Corbett's hip replacement operation, Mr. Marvin's diabetes, Mr. Kennedy's triple bypass.

It seems to her, listening to him, that the cars are in better shape than the owners, that her father knows this and that it is part of his fascination with their world, a kind of soap opera he is happy to watch, even visit as a tourist. But, like the hockey he enjoys watching on television, it is for him a passion best lived vicariously.

She imagines how the impromptu caravan now forming on the road must look from the landscaped sidelines, imagines the stately parade of pampered automobiles with their food van bringing up the rear — faded blue, discreetly dented, tongues of rust licking at the edges. The others should be grateful, she thinks. With their van in attendance, they must look even swankier than they think.

IT WAS THE end of the term. After breakfast — she had slept late after a long night finishing her final term paper — she told her parents she would be going to the new Steven Spielberg movie with Kelly and a few of her friends. Afterwards, they planned to have dinner at a restaurant, a Mexican place known for good food and cheap prices. Since the evening would finish late, Kelly had invited her to crash in her dorm room.

Her mother, standing at the stove salting and stirring a pot of *channa dhal*, said there was no need to inconvenience Kelly, her father would be glad to come pick her up at the restaurant, she just had to call when dinner was over — and where was the restaurant, by the way?

Her father, finishing a coffee at the dining table before heading out on his lunchtime rounds, nodded. "Anytime," he said. Then, unexpectedly, he turned towards her mother. "On the other hand, she has visited Kelly's cottage. If Kelly has invited her to spend the night in her room, what harm can there be."

Later, when they met as arranged outside the university library, Kelly said, "Sue, do your parents know you're at university now?" Her Greenpeace T-shirt moulded itself around her braless breasts; her jeans, with a diamond pattern cut along the thighs, were at least two sizes too small.

"Pretty sure. They pay for it." It was a warm afternoon in late April. The trees were budding, the grass turning green.

"I mean, the way you have to sneak around, it's like you're still in high school. It's just a party, for God's sake." Blue eyeshadow sparkled on her eyelids. She had had her hair waved.

"Kel, my parents' idea of a party is a bunch of people sitting around the local temple with plates on their laps and glasses of fruit punch in their hands." Sumintra felt that, beside Kelly, she looked plain in her white cotton blouse and brown slacks.

They had an early dinner at the Mexican restaurant, a student hangout on the edge of the campus. As she dipped her tortilla chips in hot sauce and forked *refritos* and *pollo diablo* into her mouth, Sumintra kept it to herself that eating here helped soothe her conscience.

Darkness was coming on when they took the subway to the West End. The house was on a quiet residential street a short walk away from the station. Its red-brick walls and roofed wooden porch, flags hung as curtains in the win-

THE SOUL OF ALL GREAT DESIGNS

dows and a certain scruffiness in the lawn — patches of browned grass, flower beds left bare — distinguished it from its more groomed neighbours.

Kelly pressed the bell and the door opened to the screech-ing of an electric guitar and loud voices. The house was crowded. Sumintra recognized a few faces from her classes. Kelly seemed to know everyone by name. Soon, each with a beer that had been pressed on them, they were separated.

Sumintra found herself sitting on the living-room floor among a group of people engaged in a playful discussion about what should be done with the site where the towers of the World Trade Center had stood. She had no opinion, but enjoyed listening to the various ideas: the world's largest children's playground, the world's tallest skyscraper, the world's biggest swimming pool, a replica of the Auschwitz death camp, a housing development for New York's indigents, a living replica of the Guantanamo Bay detention camp.

Then she remembered the burning buildings and the bodies falling from them. The falling bodies led to the falling plane and that other Sumintra hugging her daughters to her chest.

She thought she would find another conversation to eavesdrop on.

In one corner of the living room, people were circled around an unshaven, pear-shaped man. "So you see," the man said, accepting one of the joints making the rounds, "Stalin got a bum rap." Across from them, a couple was deep in conversation, the man leaning in towards the woman who had her back to the corner. She looked trapped but not unpleasantly so. As Sumintra walked by them towards the kitchen, she saw the back of the woman's hand brush brazenly down the man's crotch, heard him say, "But of course, the London theatre scene is far more vibrant ..."

The kitchen was dense with bodies and smoke and the yap of voices. In the fibrous light, she glimpsed Kelly standing in the far corner beside the fridge. She was laughing and nodding. Sumintra began pressing through the crowd, her beer bottle held to her chest. A broad back blocked her way. She tapped on the shoulder. "S'cuse me please, just squeezing through."

The man glanced over his shoulder: dark curls plastered to his forehead, watery red eyes blinking at her. He turned to face her. "Hi, there," he said. "You look familiar. What's your name?" His breath was sour with whisky.

"Sue." She forced a smile.

"I'm Dan."

"Sorry to disturb you, Dan. I just wanted to get through —"

"You're a pretty one, aren't you. Where do I know you from?"

"Couldn't say." The stench of his breath was making her queasy. "If I could just —"

"I like your skin, Sue. Café au lait."

She didn't know what to say to this. She began looking for a way to sidle past his wide smile and narrowed eyes.

He said, "Let's find a bedroom so's I can drink some, what d'you say?"

It seemed to her that all conversation in the kitchen stopped at that moment, that there was nothing left but his crude suggestion and the slits of his eyes and the tip of his tongue emerging wet from between his lips.

From the void that opened up within her, she said, "Fuck off."

His face went blank. Then his eyes widened and she saw that they were dead. Twisting his lips as if to dispel a bad taste, he spat, "Are all Paki girls cunts like you?"

At that moment, all conversation in the kitchen really did stop. Eyes flickered towards them. The silence formed an arena, Sumintra at its centre, the audience awaiting her response. She worked her tongue searching for saliva to spit at him but her mouth was dry with fear.

Seconds later, his friends, mouthing apologies, were dragging him away and Kelly was putting her arm around her and leading her through the parting crowd out to the backyard. "He's just a fucking creep, an asshole," Kelly said, trying to persuade her to stay. Finally, she gave her the room keys, said she didn't expect to be back tonight.

On her way back to the subway, Sue replayed the conversation again and again. The first of his hateful words — an import from England, strangely alien and without bite here — was easy to dismiss. But she found herself tripping over the second. She brought it to her tongue, whispered it to herself. *Cunt.* She whispered it again, noticing its shape, noting the hardness of the consonants at the beginning and the end, the softness of the connecting vowel like a polite cough. Then she repeated the word again and again, like a mantra, and by the time she inserted her token into the turnstile she had washed it of his venom. When the subway train hissed into the station, the word — forbidden, tantalizing — led her to wonder what she might have done had he been less uncouth, less reptilian, charming. As the train rumbled through the dark tunnel, she remade him: brightening his eyes, softening his lips, sweetening his words, causing curls to fall pleasingly onto his forehead.

The next evening, alone at home while her parents were at dinner at the Kumars, she dug out Kelly's gift from the bottom of her desk drawer. She removed the batteries from her portable CD player and inserted them into the vibrator. Then she lay back naked on her bed with the reading light on above her desk and, to the soft buzzing sound, thought of the man she had moulded who liked her café au lait skin.

Afterwards, as the tingle receded from her flesh, she began to understand that she was more thrilled by the idea of transgression than by transgression itself.

THE GATHERINGS, HER father has explained, are organized but informal, the occasion social rather than commercial. The Classic Car Association makes arrangements with small towns or shopping centres for appropriate spaces — the local fairground, perhaps, or a closed-off section of a parking lot — and publishes the dates and addresses in the trade magazines. Often they enlist the local Scouts to direct traffic. Whoever wishes to can come and park his vehicle for the admiration of others. Sometimes deals are made but more often advice is dispensed, leads are given for rare parts, prizes are awarded for work well done. They are on the whole not an envious bunch, these classic-car owners.

Early every spring, her father buys the trade magazines and highlights in yellow the weekend gatherings in their vicinity. A methodical man, he then locates the various towns on a road map of the province, plots out the most direct route, works out the mileage, the driving time and the cost of gas, and chooses which are worth his while against expected revenues. The day before the gathering, he checks the weather forecast. If rain is predicted, attendance will be sparse and those who do turn out will be unlikely to hang around for long, so more often than not he cancels the outing and gets a little extra sleep. This means that, on those mornings when she is supposed to accompany him to lend a hand, she too can get a little extra sleep. Last night she checked the weather channel before going to bed. A glorious day ahead. Damn.

Her father follows Mr. Kennedy's black Cadillac onto the exit for Lambton. Up ahead she sees the steeple of a small church, grey-green hills rising on the horizon.

Lambton. She hasn't been here before but as they drive along the main street — along with the church, a one-pump service station, a small grocery store advertising video rentals and a special on cigarettes, ramshackle antique shops, houses so neat and hermetic she finds it impossible to summon images of the lives within — it looks to her like one of dozens of such places dotted throughout the countryside. They are places, she feels, which can be known only from the outside, their references to people and events inaccessible to those who have not made their lives there. It is the kind of place that feels vaguely threatening.

Her father says the gathering is to be held in a park on the other side of town. "It is called Centennial Park," he says, "a gift from the government five years ago to celebrate their founding." As usual, he has done his homework, and more. "What a young country we live in, daughter!"

The town ends at a grey Quonset hut set back from the road. On its packed-earth yard scored by deep tire tracks sits a small tractor and a hill of honey-coloured sand that mimics the shape of the hut. Just ahead, past an unpaved road leading away from the main road, begins the park. At a glance, she sees that it is the grandest thing about

Lambton: the lawn green and lush and newly mowed, stands of shade trees with wrought-iron benches placed at the base, discreet cobbled paths leading to brick barbecue pits. Beyond the first stands of trees, lined up on the lawn, are the cars, glittering and colourful, convertibles with their roofs retracted. Owners, the men for the most part in jeans and T-shirts, the women in slacks or sundresses, are gathered in small groups, chatting. Others are peering at upholstery or into engine wells, or running chamois cloths along the chassis and chrome bumpers.

Her father spots a space across from what he says is a '56 Buick Century. A couple of men wave at him in greeting. He says, "Mr. Dooling in the white shirt, '38 Cadillac Lasalle, diabetic but a marathon runner, and that's Mr. Alberts with him, '59 Ford Skyliner, no medical problems I know of. Mr. Dooling will be here in two-twos for a coffee, black, and Mr. Alberts will be with him for a double-double." He gives a robust tug on the handbrake and turns the engine off.

ON THE TELEPHONE, Kelly said, "Sue, you've got to come. It's my first apartment."

At dinner that evening, her mother said, "Party? What kind of party?"

"A housewarming, graduation kind of party, Mamu."

Her mother, Sumintra learnt young, was a back-seat driver, not in the van but in life. She anticipated the worst for

herself and for others so that the worst could be avoided
— and, if not avoided, then dealt with when it came crashing down. It was one of that other Sumintra's legacies.

Her father, absorbed in the newspaper folded in two
beside his plate, said, "Where is this apartment?"

"Downtown, Papu, just west of the financial district. It's
a safe area."

Her mother, filling their glasses with iced water, said,
"Why doesn't Kelly live with her parents instead? She will
save her money, no rent to pay, like you."

"That's her business, Mamu. We're not students anymore, she's got a full-time job. Besides, maybe her parents
don't want her living with them."

"Why not? What's wrong with her?"

"What a question, Mamu! Kelly's my friend. There's
nothing wrong with her. It's just the way things are here.
They're not like us, the kids living with the parents till
they get married. It's just a different way of doing things,
that's all."

Her father said, "Is it an apartment building with a
proper security system or a flat in one of those old houses
where anybody can just walk in off the street willy-nilly?"

He slid the newspaper across the table towards her.
A black-and-white photo showed a room in shambles:
a house party that had got out of hand thanks to a swarm
of uninvited guests. Somebody had ended up getting
stabbed.

She slid the paper back towards him. "Papu, this was in the East End and, besides, Kelly's very careful."

Her mother, spooning tamarind chutney from a bottle, said, "You can't be careful enough. Just the other day, Mrs. Kumar was telling me about a man they had to chase away from their park — all those little children playing on the swings and the slides and whatnot, and this man, he comes and exposes himself! Can you imagine! The mothers raised a hullabaloo and he skedaddled off but those poor children, marked for life by a man who likes to show off his big engine!"

Sumintra saw her father's lips twitch. She said, "How do you know it was a big engine, Mamu?"

Her father kept his eyes riveted on the newspaper but his lips began trembling in amusement. Her mother's face clouded over. "Big engine, small engine, what does it matter? He wanted to show it off most inappropriately! Manohar! Forget the newspaper and talk sense to your daughter."

Her father raised his eyes towards the ceiling. "Four-cylinder, six-cylinder — this is all beside the point. My wife, I fail to see what this has to do with Sumintra's going to Kelly's party. Where's the harm? One day, sooner rather than later we hope, she will be married and she will go wherever she pleases. If she wishes to go to Kelly's housewarming, I see no harm in that. They are both trustworthy young ladies."

"At least let us have her phone number," her mother said, her fingers dipping into the wooden box where she kept the trail mix of pills with which she began and ended her days.

"It hasn't been hooked up yet." She didn't bother to mention Kelly's cellphone.

When her father offered to drop her off at Kelly's new place, Sumintra couldn't refuse. She suspected she would have had to take the bus and subway had he not wanted to check out the building for himself.

When they pulled up at the curb in front of the apartment tower, his neck craning forward to eye the twenty stories of chrome and glass through the dusty windshield, he said, "Come home in one piece, daughter, or your mother will never forgive me."

She opened the door of the van, slung the overnight bag onto her shoulder. "See you tomorrow, Papu. Don't worry."

"I always worry, daughter. Worry, as you will one day find out, God willing, is part of a parent's tool kit."

The next day, when she returned home, her mother leaned close and sniffed her blouse. "It smells like smoke," she said.

"There were a few smokers at the party."

Her mother's brow furrowed. "It doesn't smell like tobacco. It is quite pleasant, actually."

"They were from France. They were smoking French cigarettes, Mamu."

"Well," her mother said, taking the overnight bag from her, "at least French cigarettes smell more pleasant than the ones people smoke here."

Sumintra excused herself. The last guests had left around three that morning, she said, and since she was to sleep on the sofa in the living room her night had been short. She wanted to take a shower, have a nap — and avoid her mother's questions. That way she wouldn't have to be vigilant about slips of the tongue. Her mother would never know what the pleasant French tobacco really was or that a neighbour had complained about the noise or that she had drunk too much wine or that her lack of sleep was due to lying agitated on the sofa for what seemed like an eternity listening to Kelly and her new boyfriend make noisy love behind the closed bedroom door.

She would take a long shower and slip naked between the sheets of her bed, the vibrator buzzing as she remembered the wet, gasping sounds and the heaving of breath that had come from Kelly's bedroom — and one particular man with steel-grey eyes and thin lips, a colleague of Kelly's who, to Sue's fanciful regret, had brought his wife along.

BUSINESS IS BRISK for the next hour or so as customers form two lines at the van, Sumintra serving one, her father the other. Sandwiches, chips, chocolate bars, coffee and soft drinks. Several times her father slips around to the other side of the van to fill white plastic cups with beer. A little boy begins to cry when he's told there are no hot dogs but he goes off smiling when Sumintra offers him a free bag of licorice nubs. A few men try to offer her a tip and they seem confused when she refuses. She has the curious impression that the women don't see her at all, they look right through her. Mr. Alberts returns for a second double-double. He is a short, compact man with wavy silvered hair and mischievous eyes. As she hands him a stir stick and napkin, he says, "Manny's a lucky man. Such a young and beautiful wife!"

"I'm not his wife," she says. "I'm his daughter." Quickly, she adds: "But thanks for the compliment anyway."

His widening smile reveals teeth too perfect, too white, to be natural. "Either way," he says, "Manny's a lucky man."

Her father, who has overheard the conversation, says, "And he knows it too, Mr. Alberts, sir."

Later, as they drive home in the softened afternoon sun, her father will tell her that Mr. Alberts, in his younger days, was something of a ladies' man. According to the stories he likes to spin, he was quite successful thanks to his humour and flirtatiousness and his ability to cut a rug to the sounds of his favourite crooners. Then he fell head-over-heels in love, married and enjoyed a childless, ten-year marriage until his wife keeled over from a heart attack one day while he was at work. He found her lying on the living-room rug when he returned home that evening. Her father will tell her that when he relates that story, Mr. Alberts' eyes water even though his wife died over twenty-five years ago. All of this he learnt last summer while examining Mr. Alberts' '59 Ford Skyliner. Sumintra, listening to her father as the landscape peels by, will be struck that he, too, is moved by the story, just as she is struck by the language he uses — *cut a rug, crooners, head-over-heels, keel over* — language that is not his own but that has been given to him by Mr. Alberts. She admires his ability to absorb influence from the world around him. It is not one her mother shares — her world barely extends beyond home and the temple community — and Sumintra will be warmed by the thought that she has inherited this trait from him.

Her father sighs. "Poor Mr. Alberts. Fate is cruel sometimes, daughter. How does a man survive when his wife disappears, just like that?"

"But Papu," she says with surprise, "it happens all the time." She doesn't have to pronounce Sumintra's name, or the names of her daughters. She does not dare pronounce that other name, the one that haunts her even more than her namesake.

NEIL BISSOONDATH

HER NAME WAS Rima and she no longer lives here. At least that's what they say. She was one of those girls — tall, slender, with waist-long hair — who always seemed to be bustling along the halls of their high school. They never spoke, which Sumintra now vaguely regrets. They should have been friends, even though Rima's family was from Bombay. Mutual acquaintances claimed they had so much in common. This was perhaps why Sumintra and Rima never made a move to get to know each other: *so much in common* was itself a kind of barrier. Sumintra was drawn to people who were as unlike herself as possible.

Still, she knew the basic facts about Rima. They had progressed together through high school, in the same grade but always in different classes. Their parents had arrived within months of each other. Her parents — her father was an electrical engineer with Hydro, her mother an obstetrician whose qualifications and experience, it was said, had been made useless by immigration — had opened up a successful Indian restaurant in the mall serving their subdivision. At school Rima acquired a reputation. She was known for her intelligence, her social skills, her quiet elegance. If Rima wore a new hairpin one day, half the girls in their grade would be wearing it within a week. She was elected student-council president and collected commendations for community work, and trophies for track, public speaking and science-fair projects. She was captain of the volleyball and soccer teams. Everyone knew she would one day find a cure for cancer or write a bestselling novel or mount an Olympic podium. There were so many reasons for Sumintra to avoid her.

The summer after the end of high school, Rima's absence was noticed — a final gathering in late August before everyone scattered to various universities. Rima never turned up and no one seemed to know why. Someone had heard she'd gone to Bombay for the summer. *No*, someone else said, *France*. Her absence put a damper on the party, several girls drifted away early.

Sumintra was at the shopping mall a few weeks later looking for sales on summer blouses when she ran into Kayla, whom she remembered from high school for the sole reason that Kayla had boasted to anyone who would listen about having had sex. Kayla, whose shoulder-length hair now sported the colours of the rainbow, had decided to become a hair-and-nail stylist. Content to leave behind an uninspired period of her life, Sumintra hadn't kept in touch with anyone and was about to flee Kayla's yammering when Kayla said, "Hey, did you hear about Rima?"

AT THE DINNER table that evening, Sumintra said, "Hey guys, remember —"

"We are not guys," her mother snapped.

"Sorry, Mamu."

"Your father is here too."

"Sorry, Papu."

Her father, fingering rice into a ball, said, "It's all right, daughter. I am a guy."

Her mother narrowed her eyes at him. "You want to be a guy for your daughter? Fine, then, go ahead. Be a guy — but not in my house. What next? You will be letting her run around with BMWs?"

"Our daughter runs around with nobody. She is a good girl." He popped the rice ball into his mouth, the hum of an unrecognizable song rising from his throat as he chewed, an unmistakable sign that he was enjoying his meal.

Sumintra glanced from her father to her mother and back again. How in the world had they slid from her slip of the tongue to the community's obsession with protecting their daughters from Blacks, Muslims and Whites?

Her mother patted at her heaving chest as if to assure her panicked heart that all was well. "You are right," she said more quietly. "Our Sumintra is a good girl." She turned towards her, forced a smile. "So, what were you going to say?"

"It's nothing."

"Nobody begins saying something about nothing, Sumintra. What is it?"

Sumintra crossed her knife and fork on her plate and rested one hand on top of the other. "Well, remember that girl Rima I used to go to school with?"

"Acha!" her mother said. "What a pile of trouble she was, that one. Her poor parents!"

Her father grunted, gazed at the new rice ball he was shaping with his fingers.

Sumintra said, "No, no. This Rima was the star of the school. She won every prize going. Even the principal thought she was Queen Bee."

Her father said, "Are you talking about Dr. Prasad's daughter?" His eyes remained anchored to his plate.

"Right. That Rima."

"What about her?" her mother said cautiously, laying both hands flat beside her plate.

"There's a rumour going around that her parents have packed her off to India, for good. You know anything about that?"

"Idle gossip," her mother said. "You must not be paying attention to such things."

"But nobody's seen her since graduation. She was supposed to be studying chemistry or something at U of T."

"This is Mr. Prasad and Dr. Prasad's business. You must not go sticking your nose up other people's business, Sumintra."

"*In* other people's business," her father said.

"They say she got into some trouble and her parents —"

"Enough, Sumintra! Mr. and Dr. Prasad are good people. They come to temple every week. Dr. Prasad supplies food at discount to the less fortunate members of the community. I will not have you talking —"

"And why not?" her father said sharply. He abandoned

his rice ball in the middle of his plate. "Why not? Everybody at temple knows what happened. Sumintra should know. Their honour was at stake, and the honour of our community. They could not let it pass."

Her mother was silent for a moment. "Of course not, husband. They could not let it pass. They had to be acting."

"So will you tell Sumintra or will I?"

Sumintra, cautious, said, "So the rumours are true?"

"I don't know about the rumours," her mother said. "I only know what happened."

Sumintra waited as her parents silently negotiated who would tell her.

Her mother took a sip of water, patted her lips. "Mr. and Dr. Prasad discovered that Rima was in touch with a boy, a boy they did not know."

"So what's wrong with that?"

"A white boy. Jewish to boot."

"At school I know all kinds of guys."

"But, daughter, this boy was not just a friend to Rima. They wrote love letters to each other. Who knows what other disgusting things they were up to. Her parents pleaded with her to stop but she would not listen. What are parents to do? They even locked her in her room for a whole weekend but first chance she got she skedaddled back to the boy."

"So it's true, then. They sent her back to India."

"She is with family there. They will find her a suitable husband."

"So what's to stop her from hopping a plane back?"

"How will she get a ticket? They have taken away her passport too. It is here, she is there."

"She's got rights."

"She has two citizenships, daughter, just like you," her father said, leaning back in his chair. "There she is Indian. This country can do nothing for her. Besides, it would be a foolish thing for her to be trying to do. The consequences ... For us, disobedience is not a joke, it is a kind of betrayal." He pushed his plate away, placed his elbows on the table and folded his hands together. "They had to protect the family's honour. It is not like here. A child does something bad and the parents can still hold their heads high." He took a deep breath, cleared his throat. "It is known in our community, daughter, that some families have gone much further than Mr. and Dr. Prasad. A man can be driven to physical violence against those he loves most when they betray him. Usually it is hushed up. We hate to wash our dirty laundry in public. But that dirty laundry must be dealt with. Mr. and Dr. Prasad dealt with it in the most humane way possible. Nobody can fault them for that, daughter."

"Why couldn't they just let her alone? It's her life. Seems to me the best way to live your life is to know and accept yourself, then just go on from there."

Her mother's eyelids fluttered in disquiet. "What about finding a husband?"

"You hope that life brings you someone who gets to know you and accepts you as you are." Sumintra knew her words were heresy, but confirmation of Rima's fate had made her angry and fearful.

Her mother glanced away in dismissal, her lips pursed, her cheeks quivering.

Her father said, "This is not our way, daughter. Leaving things to chance, perhaps yes, perhaps no. You would not be here now if our parents had not brought your mother and me together."

"Parents have a responsibility, Sumintra," her mother said. "Mr. and Dr. Prasad could not just sit back and watch their daughter ruin her life and theirs. As your Papu said, this is not our way. Now finish your dinner. It is getting cold."

Sumintra picked up her knife in one hand, then she picked up her fork in the other. For a brief moment, she didn't know what they were for.

BUSINESS EVENTUALLY SLACKS off. They have done well. Her father, satisfied, neatens the stack of bills and folds it in two. Leaving enough in the cash box for her to make change, he inserts the money deep into his pants pocket and does up the button meant to outwit pickpockets —

her mother's idea. He takes a cigarette from the glove compartment and secures it above his ear. "I will make the rounds, daughter."

From a compartment in the van she takes out a folding canvas chair and the fat paperback she leaves there for these quiet moments. She uncaps a bottle of water and begins to read, sliding easily into the travails of life in Bombay. The novel is entertaining, soap-operatic; it makes no demand on her intellect, like the Agatha Christies and Raymond Chandlers. In the silence, among the words flowing effort-lessly through her mind, she becomes aware of birds chirping in the trees and of the gentle clasp of warmth on her skin. She is glad to be here among strangers, with no responsibility other than the occasional simple commercial exchange. *Here are your chips, here's your change. Can I get you anything else? Thanks. You're welcome.*

"Uh, excuse me, miss?"

She looks up and closes the book. The man standing before her is tall and lanky, with closely trimmed brown hair and soft eyes. He's slightly younger than most of the people here — in his early thirties, perhaps, mid-thirties at the most — and not bad-looking, despite the earring in his right ear. Getting to her feet, she says, "Hi, what can I get you?"

"I don't suppose you can manage a glass of red wine?" He's wearing a lemon-coloured polo shirt, tan pants, and loafers.

She laughs. "'Fraid not." She doesn't mention the beer; they are only for her father's regulars, people who won't tattle, and she doesn't know if he's a regular.

"Maybe just some water then." He takes a change purse from his pocket and dips his thumb and forefinger into it.

Something about the gesture, something in the tenor of his voice: *Too bad*, Sumintra thinks as she hands him the cold bottle of water. Accepting his money, she says, "Which one's yours?"

"Pardon?"

"Which car?"

"Oh." He looks away to the shiny automobiles and the people milling about among the trees. Then he turns back to face her. "None, actually."

"You window-shopping?" His eyes prompt a surge of warmth in her chest, a light commotion in her belly.

"You could say so." He unscrews the top from the bottle, takes a long drink. "I'm working on a '29 Chevrolet Sedan but it'll be a while before it's ready to be shown." The tips of his fingers pat lightly at a drop of water on his lower lip.

"What do you do when you're not working on the Chevrolet?" She becomes aware of a kind of acceleration within her, curiosity materializing of its own volition. She's never felt this before: a commotion, an internal volatility.

"I'm a house painter," he says. "I have my own company."

"You don't look like a house painter."

"What does a house painter look like?"

"I don't know. Not like you. But I mean it as a compliment." She hears the words falling from her tongue, words unconsidered, unexamined for potential reactions. Part of her is thrilled by her daring, part of her is scandalized by it.

"I'll take it as a compliment, then." His lips twitch in a light smile that suggests he is amused by more than just their conversation — that she has engaged something deeper within him too.

Adrenaline races through her veins, sparking against her nerves, bringing a breathless clarity to her mind: perhaps she has misread the gestures, the softness of his lilting voice? She suddenly has many questions she would like to ask, feels impelled to ask him to stay longer, to sit with her, talk.

She knows it is what Kelly would do.

But she knows too — and she is engulfed by its sheer weight — that it is not what Sumintra would do.

Aching with disappointment at herself, she says, "Will there be anything else?"

He shakes his head. "Thanks, uhh — what's your name?"

"Sue."

"Thanks, Sue." He screws the top back onto the bottle.

"What's yours?" she blurts out.

"You can call me Alec."

"Alex?"

"No, Alec. With a C."

"Nice chatting with you, Alec with a C."

"You, too." He turns to go. Then he stops, turns back to face her.

Part Three

She calls me "Alec," a name that came to me out of the clear blue sky that hot afternoon in a park in some small town — Crowfield, I think, or perhaps it was Lambton. Somewhere in that area, not that it matters. I've got used to the name. *Alec.* Even grown fond of it. It's got snap and personality. It suggests new traits to explore.

I'd had lunch in the town, something Italian — not a memorable meal, or at least memorable only because it was too salty and the wine had been indifferent. The search for antiques hadn't been particularly fruitful, but the folks at the restaurant tipped me off to a farmer a few kilometres down the highway who'd sold out to a conglomerate and was preparing to get rid of his stuff. Most of the farm equipment was already spoken for, but he had a houseful of furniture that had been in his family for generations. They gave me his number and lent me their phone. A tired-sounding man said he'd be expecting me towards the end of the afternoon. With a couple of hours to kill in a one-traffic-light town, I was lucky that a group of vintage-car enthusiasts were holding a get-together in the local park.

The Chevy had sat in my garage through the winter, untouched for long stretches of time. Closer inspection of the body confirmed it was in good shape, just the few dents and a half-dozen discreet colonies of rust. Replacing the flaking rubber on the running boards was simple, but stripping off the old paint had taken me weeks of a few hours here and there. It was tedious work.

A mechanic had checked out the engine. After a visual inspection and a bit of tugging at this and pushing at that — "Looks pretty good for an old-timer," he said — he put in some gas and had no trouble starting it up. Only one cylinder was running, though, so he tapped the valves, sprayed on some anti-rust and they freed up. The radiator was in fine shape but, after all those years in storage, things like the spark plugs, points and condenser needed replacing. The transmission and brakes were in fairly good condition, and the head and tail lights worked — but the horn didn't, of all things. Mechanically, the car was in pretty good shape. The mechanic, who repaired machinery for one of my regular contractors, did the work quickly, efficiently and discreetly — he pocketed a good wad of cash that went a long way in paying off his gambling debts. We agreed there was no need for his boss or the tax people to know about it.

The biggest challenge was going to be the interior frame. It was made of wood, and the slats of white ash had rotted. I'd secured a supply of the wood and, with patience and my carpentry skills, began the task of remaking from scratch practically all the pieces — the front and rear door pillars, the roof and floor rails, the roof bows, a new floorboard for the front. Precision was everything if the body was to fit snugly on the frame when I put it back in place. There was the sanding and priming and painting, all the chrome to refinish, and new tires and various trimmings to order from parts suppliers in Pennsylvania and Arizona. If it weren't a labour of love, it would have been just plain old labour — and at times it was just that. Still, it suited me. It required thought, planning, organization and the patience to concentrate on one area at a time so as to avoid feeling overwhelmed by all that needed doing — always keeping in mind the larger picture, the ultimate goal, allowing nothing to push me off course, not my own weaknesses, not external pressures.

I'd subscribed to a variety of car magazines for technical information and ideas. They often ran notices for various exhibitions and rallies, but I'd never managed to make it to one. It was a pleasant way to spend the time, walking around the park — an example of my tax dollars at work — examining the vintage cars, admiring the care that had gone into their restoration, chatting with the proud owners, who were happy to share their enthusiasm and the details, sometimes painfully minute, of the hundreds of hours they'd lavished on their hobby. Without exception, they disdained cheating, only original parts would do. Kits, one man said dismissively, were like a woman with a tit-job — even if her breasts were perfect, there was no getting away from the fact that they were fakes. Or like instant coffee, said his friend twirling an empty coffee cup between his fingers and chewing on a stir stick — it'd do in a pinch but without the flavour of the real thing. Another man, showing off his car's yellowing registration papers — a succession of owners in Akron, Bangor, Daytona Beach, Montreal and a couple of other places — said that a car without a history was like a guy with amnesia, something essential was missing. The depth of their passion heartened me and I decided then and there to cut no corners and make no compromises with my Chevy.

After a while, the salty food and hot afternoon made me thirsty. The man with the coffee cup directed me to a food truck. A young woman was sitting on a chair beside it, reading. As I approached, she glanced up, her black hair catching a shimmer of sunlight. My breath seized. I had seen more beautiful women, yes, sexier women, women whose eyes could stop a conversation, whose smiles could muddle thought. But I'd never come face to face with a woman whose very being literally took my breath away. She stood up, graceful and lean in her cotton blouse and jeans. She was of average height, with dark eyes, her hair falling well below her shoulders. When she asked what I wanted, I mumbled something stupid about wine. My answer made her laugh and I was captivated, utterly, terrifyingly. There was a strange perfection to her features — a centimetre this way or that would have rendered her ordinary, but those centimetres had fallen in her favour. I asked for a bottle of water, hoping as I dug out my change that I could turn and walk away and spend the next few hours trying to forget that I'd seen her, had reacted to her in a way that profoundly challenged me, in a way I hadn't since Caroline.

She engaged me in conversation, an exchange of pleasantries I happily went along with above the drumming of my heart. She asked my name. Alec came to me. Then the conversation came to a natural end and I managed to turn to go, my mind instructing my body to do what neither of them wished to.

I don't know what caused me to hesitate. It was as if her intensity — and it wasn't anything you could put your finger on, it was just there like some kind of mystery braided around the most innocuous of her words — as if this intensity was too much to resist, washing over me and overwhelming my better judgement. I stopped, turned, and saw she'd been waiting for me to do just that.

Having survived Caroline, I wasn't in the market for another near-death experience. But the damned things have a way of creeping up on you.

She agreed to dinner the following Friday. I asked for her phone number, she asked for mine. Neither of us would give it — her reluctance intrigued me — but after a minute of puzzled silence, she ripped a blank page from the end of her book and wrote down her address. I would pick her up at seven.

In a way that Caroline would never have wanted to, Sue — brown-skinned, dark-haired, dark-eyed Sue — was destined to become one of my secrets. And I, without my suspecting it, was destined to become one of hers.

A HAZE HAD settled on the city, a soup of brownish chemicals so dense the radio had been broadcasting warnings to people with respiratory and heart ailments to stay indoors. I'd spent the afternoon solving supply problems — a constant in my business — and looking for ways to accelerate the work on a job that had fallen behind schedule. At some point, the air conditioning in the office had given out, and by the time I left the office to pick up my rental car — a design team that would be working late would lock up — my temples were throbbing and my mood matched the grim sky. My disposition wasn't helped by a growing conviction that Sue — if that was really her name — had played a trick on me. Her address would turn out to be phony or no one there would ever have heard of her.

After picking up the car, I drove home, popped some pills for the headache and took a long, cool shower. Standing under the pouring faucet, I decided that I wouldn't be made a fool of. She was good-looking, but not that good. As for the magnetism I'd felt, surely that had been because of the bad meal, the heat, my thirst — nothing but a kind of light-headedness due to dehydration.

And yet, as I stretched out on my bed and closed my eyes, the memory of that feeling returned only slightly diminished: it still had the power to make my heart race.

I turned onto my side, pushed the feeling away. The world, I thought, was full of temptation and this Sue was one of mine. There was a lot at stake, too much to risk. In my line of work, reputation is everything and my reputation had been built around the image I'd created so successfully that my company had been asked to sponsor a float in the city's gay pride parade. Convinced that, in Sue, I was flirting with danger, I decided to check into a hotel and call up the agency to see who was available. Maybe they would have some brown-skinned, dark-haired, dark-eyed lady who could help me lance my memory of Sue. The headache was proving stubborn but I was determined that the evening wouldn't be a total loss.

It was only as I was crawling along in the Friday evening stop-and-go traffic downtown that it occurred to me that I wasn't far from the address Sue had written down. I took out the page I'd folded into my wallet. It was only a couple of blocks away and, at this pace, I would go past it at just after seven. Despite myself, I felt a flutter of excitement. What if she ...? Should I ...? But no. As my father had once said, you can get the most beautiful view from the edge of a cliff, but only a fool would jump off.

I switched on the radio. The seven o'clock news breathlessly announced "a breaking story" — police raids on East End massage parlours had netted two dozen Chinese and Eastern-European illegals. This was followed by unconfirmed reports — "details are still sketchy" — of a drive-by shooting in the North End. The news reader was reporting on the ongoing investigation into the kidnapping and murder of a toddler, when the traffic flow picked up, and there, half a block down the street on my right, was the new chrome-and-glass apartment building Sue claimed as her address. And there, too, standing in front of the smoked-glass entrance, looking almost lost among the passing crowds, was Sue. She was wearing a blue sundress with white moons printed on it and her hair was falling loose about her shoulders. In her hands she clutched a white handbag.

In the minute it took me to manoeuvre the car over to the curb through a din of protesting car horns, my headache vanished.

———

IF HER PARENTS call — they are unlikely to do so, but she is careful to anticipate the unlikely — Kelly will say that Sue has developed a migraine — the bad air, probably — and that she's taken some tablets and is sleeping it off in the bedroom. She expects she will sleep right through the night and will call them back tomorrow — or should she go wake her? Sumintra knows her parents, knows they will say no, no, let her sleep, tomorrow morning will be fine.

Buckling the seat belt, she says, "I wasn't sure you'd come." She sniffles, her nose irritated by the fumes she's been breathing for almost fifteen minutes. The car smells new.

Signalling and pulling back out into the traffic, Alec says, "I wasn't sure about you either. I started thinking it was kind of crazy, my suddenly asking you out like that."

"Are you sorry you did?"

"I'm here, aren't I? But I was sure you'd think I was some kind of maniac, out to kidnap you."

The thought has occurred to her and, several times through the week, she has resolved to be sitting in a cinema with a bag of popcorn at 7:00 p.m. on Friday.

She called Kelly and she, too, was suspicious. An utter stranger, perhaps gay or, at least, on the effeminate side: She counselled caution. Of course, she herself has left bars with men met just hours before but, still, that was after a lot of talk, drinks, time enough to size them up. On the other hand, sometimes the gut just gets the message instantaneously — take her boyfriend, for instance. There was every reason in the world not to get involved with him. He was older, he was divorced, he was on medication for clinical depression. She should have run in the opposite direction. But her instinct had seen beyond all that. It had told her there was something worth pursuing — and no, she wasn't talking about his successful law practice or his sailboat. So far, so good. Her instinct hadn't misled her. Only Sue could know how far to trust her mind, how far to trust her instinct. After a few seconds of silence — she could hear Kelly's radio blaring in the background — she asked if she could sleep at her place on Friday night.

Following the traffic, he eases the car up a big exit ramp, past the baseball stadium and the concrete communications tower soaring beside it, and onto the highway that follows the lake out of town. A series of billboards flash by as the traffic speeds up: a rock station, a car company, a TV news show, the time in yellow blinking to the temperature in red ...

She says, "Are you a maniac?"

"Most people would say I'm not. But that doesn't mean I'm not out to entrap you."

His candour relaxes her. Her tension ebbs and she begins enjoying what feels now like an adventure. "So where are we going?"

"You like Italian food?"

"Who doesn't?"

"There's a little inn just on the other side of Martinville, set in a bay overlooking the lake. Food's not bad but just the view from the dining room's worth the drive."

"Do you mean the Venezia?"

"You've been there?" He speeds up, changing lanes, hurtling past the slower traffic.

Kelly's parents had organized a graduation dinner at the Venezia, family and a few friends.

"Once. You're right about the food, and the view."

She remembers a cozy lounge where they were served plates of prosciutto and bruschetta and glasses of Prosecco, toasts to Kelly and — not really an afterthought — to her, and a dinner served in the adjacent dining room with large picture windows looking out onto greenery, cascades of rock, the lake turning turquoise in the evening light. At one point, Kelly's father whispered to her that the Venezia was a family restaurant — that the maître d' was the father Kostas, that mama Eleni was the cook, that sons Nikos and Lakis were the waiters. "Not an Italian family, mind you," he said, and winked. Perhaps that explained the food.

Alec says, "Would you rather go somewhere else?" He sounds a little put out.

"No, there'll be fine, really."

As they leave the city behind, the traffic grows lighter, the air less oppressive. Alec says, "So tell me about yourself."

Tell me about yourself: a big question. She shifts in her seat, wondering where to begin, what is safe to include, what is best left out. Outside, twilight is slowly overtaking the sky and as she edits the facts of her life, a wayward thought points out that she has scarcely glanced at him since getting into the car.

KOSTAS, MORE ROTUND than she remembers, shows them to a table in the corner beside the window. He offers them each a glass of Prosecco, compliments of the house, and replaces the little oil lamp whose wick will not co-operate.

Sitting across from Alec, Sue notices that he quickly, almost furtively, examines the other diners in the half-filled dining room. She wonders whether he's afraid of being recognized: is he married? But there is no ring, and his tanned fingers are unblemished. They raise their glasses — "Cheers," he says — and they take a sip.

Now that she is facing him, she sees that he is perhaps not quite as handsome as she remembers but that his face is, well, sensitive, whatever that means. Something about the mouth perhaps, the set of the lips. Or maybe it's the eyes ... soft, yes, but wary too. She says, "So now that you know all about me, how about yourself?"

He leans forward, bracing his elbows on the table, fingertips playing with the stem of the wineglass. "Here's what you need to know about me," he says. "When I was a kid, my mother had a thing about good table manners, which was strange because while she wasn't a slob — she was a good mother — she was no society matron either. Still, no slurping your soup, no eating with your hands, no chewing with your mouth open, that kind of thing. No putting your elbows on the table. I never understood that one. What's wrong with putting your elbows on the table? So now that she's dead, I do it all the time."

She doesn't know what to say to this: it's too familiar to her, this idea of a life out of the parents' sight — almost in defiance of them. But she doesn't want him to know that she knows what it's like, at least not yet. Taking another sip from her glass, she says, "Do you slurp your soup now, too?"

He smiles, his shoulders relaxing. "That depends on who I'm with." He tips the glass against his lips, pours some Prosecco into his mouth, swallows. "And what about you? Do you have any bad habits?"

Behind them, a murmur of conversation dissolves into laughter, a woman's airy glee threading playfully through a man's chuckle.

Alec's question brings the image of the vibrator to Sue's mind. She shrugs. "Depends on what you consider bad. Ifigure if you enjoy putting your elbows on the table, no harm done."

He gazes steadily at her, a slow smile coming to his lips.

Taking another sip of the wine, she glances away to the trees, the rocks, the darkening lake. The Prosecco is unexpectedly potent. Already she feels it going to her head, bringing with it that breathless clarity she felt from the adrenaline last Saturday afternoon in Lambton — and all those questions that crowded into her mind, questions seeking answers to the minutiae of him, questions she now feels free to ask.

BY THE TIME she has finished her desert — tiramisu: "Did you know," he says, "that it means a pick-me-up?" — she has learnt that his favourite colour is blue, that he considers his childhood to have been a moderately happy one, that his parents are dead and his remaining family all live down east, that he was good at baseball and regrets not having gone to university, he might have made a good engineer, that he enjoys working with his hands so painting houses and doing minor repairs relaxes him, that he is not big on reading except for car magazines. He enjoys an occasional beer and movie and has never seen a play or visited a museum, although he admits to being curious about both.

By the last sip of her coffee, she has asked all her questions and has decided that, next to his eyes, his lips are his most attractive trait. They are slender, finely shaped, expressive to a point: something about them suggests they are as much gatekeepers as gateways to the words that come to him. That intrigues her. As he hands his credit card to grim, lanky Lakis, she finds herself wondering what it would be like to feel his lips pressed on hers.

———

I WASN'T EXPECTING her to invite me up for a nightcap — we would disturb her roommate, who was under the weather — and so wasn't disappointed when she didn't. Still, hoping to tease out an invitation, I said, "Are you sure it's not a boyfriend or something you're hiding up there?"

She didn't appreciate the question.

Sitting in the car in front of her apartment building, I broke the minute of uneasy silence by asking again for her phone number. She said her cell had broken that morning and she'd be getting a new one the following day. I pointed out that her number would be the same. She said she intended to change companies.

"Give me yours," she said. "I'll call you."

"I know a kiss-off when I hear one. I'm sorry you didn't have a good time."

"It's not a kiss-off. I enjoyed myself."

Without knowing why, I believed her. I had nothing to write on. "Got a piece of paper?" She held out her palm and I carefully inscribed my pseudonymous email address on it. It was the first time I touched her: the softness and warmth of the hand, the unexpected intimacy of the gesture, stirred me. My hand slid up her forearm, cupped her elbow. Her eyes rose from the letters inked onto her palm, met mine. I leaned towards her, saw her lips parting. Then, swallowing, she offered me her cheek — dry skin, yielding flesh, a hint of perfume.

Without a word, she stepped out of the car and pressed the door shut behind her.

I watched her walk to the door of the building, unlock it with a key she'd taken from her purse, and disappear inside. The sway of her dress about her hips remained with me for some time, like a phantom promise.

I put the car in gear and checked that the street, deserted now, was clear for a U-turn. Then temptation reared its head. I hesitated. It was late, but not too late to check into a hotel and call the agency.

THE SUN WOKE me the next morning with the warmth of Sue's hand still glowing in my palm, the swish of her dress brushing away the last tendrils of sleep. I'd neglected to draw the heavy blinds the night before and the room faced east. The white sheers were radiant with the rising sun. The air smelled lightly of cigarette smoke, the pillow of bleach. On the wall across from the bed hung a large mirror in a hideous gilt frame. For some inexplicable reason, it had been bolted to the wall, as if the hotel feared that some tasteless client might try to smuggle it out.

The night before, Clarisse, or whatever she called herself, had stood naked before it, fingering her dark curls into place, admiring herself, or perhaps steeling her nerves for the services she was about to render. Stretched out shirtless on the bed, I took in the butterfly tattooed on her lower back, her bronzed skin unbroken by tan lines, the quiver of her shoulder muscles as she fidgeted at her hair.

She turned around and stepped towards the bed, her breasts as bronzed as the rest of her, the hair as dark between her legs as on her head. I was immediately stirred. She smiled, said, "Like what you see?"

"Come find out."

She curled herself onto the bed beside me, unzipped my trousers and wormed her hand into my boxers. At that moment, possessed by her sure and knowing grasp, I felt the first intimations of an anger I hadn't yet recognized. An anger that was running like low-grade electricity through me, feeding the excitement ignited by this warm body pressed to mine. An anger, I understood as she drew off my pants, prompted by the abrupt denial of lips and the proffering of a neutral cheek.

As her mouth engulfed me, I knew beyond all doubt

that, had Sue kissed me, I would not be here now, my blood roiled by a fury that would keep me up half the night, dampening itself time and again and in every possible way in this hired body, only to rage again like some underground conflagration whipping to the surface.

Finally, in the early hours of the morning, the time came when my muscles could no longer respond. We were both depleted. She looked haggard and bruised, pathetic — and so, I imagine, did I. I dismissed her. The night had been an expensive one for me, a lucrative if occasionally painful one for her.

Lying in the searing, joyless light the following morning, remembering what she'd looked like while fixing her hair in the mirror, I searched myself for embers of the anger. I found none and dared to hope that what had survived the night was that warmth in my palm and the memory of the swirling dress. Daring to hope, too, that Sue would send a message, I checked out quickly and hurried home. I hadn't even paused to shower.

SORRY, YOU DON'T *have any new mail.*

Was I disappointed? A little. But it was still early, and she was probably asleep.

I showered the night off my body and, after some cereal and a couple of cups of strong coffee, spent the rest of the morning in the garage with the Chevy, fitting the new wooden ribs — they had to be near perfect so that when it came time to attach the various parts of the body they would be flush. It was exacting work. When I grew tired of it, I dealt with a few rust spots.

Working with the hands frees the mind. Sanding away rust or oiling parts often allowed me to find solutions to various professional problems posed by my more demanding clients — ideas and concepts that would materialize out of nowhere. Often I found the answer to a problem by ignoring it — or not quite ignoring it but not centring on it, going around the periphery, letting the ungrasped logic sort itself out.

That morning, though, my mind couldn't disengage. Sue kept intruding. I tried listening to music on the radio but that helped only a little.

When I went up for lunch, I forced myself to prepare a sandwich before going to the computer. Sandwich in hand, I checked the screen.

Sorry, you don't have any new mail.

I realized that the night hadn't snuffed out my anger after all.

———

ON MONDAY MORNING, her mother tells her that old Mr. Sieunarine, a temple devotee, has died. It isn't wholly unexpected, he's been in ill health for some time, but still, he was a good man, never missed a puja and, despite his frailty, could always be counted on to lend a helping hand. "You remember Mr. Sieunarine, don't you? He lost a grand daughter in the bombing."

The bombing: this is how her mother always refers to the attack that killed that other Sumintra and her daughters. The bombing — as if there were only one.

"He had a glass eye, remember? He used to take it out and scare you and the other children with it."

She doesn't remember Mr. Sieunarine or his glass eye but she pretends that she does, otherwise her mother will be miffed.

Her mother is going to assist the family. There is much to be done. She will be gone for the day.

Sumintra says, "Poor old guy. Give them my condolences." She does not ask whether he will be cremated with the glass eye or without. Her mother wouldn't appreciate the question.

Wrapping a veil around her head, her mother says, "Maybe you would like to come? I'm sure your presence will bring comfort to the family."

"I don't think so, Mamu. I'd be like some stranger walking in from off the street, don't you think?"

"You are my daughter. It would be a sign of respect."

Sumintra has no wish to start dissecting the meaning of respect with her mother. They have done it before: her mother's understanding of the concept is much larger, much stricter, than her own. At her wedding, she had kissed her mother-in-law's feet. She says, "You better get going, Mamu. Mr. and Mrs. Kumar are waiting for you."

Mr. and Mrs. Kumar wave at her from their car when she accompanies her mother to the door. She waves back, watches her mother get into the back seat and then locks the door. She goes to her bedroom, turns on her computer.

She has followed Kelly's advice even though she's not sure it's a good idea. Yes, she is disappointed that Alec meekly accepted her cheek, that he wasn't a little more insistent, but she'd had a good time and wanted to see him again. Would making him sweat for a few days really make him more assertive? It was only their first date, after all. Truth to tell, she hadn't planned to turn her lips away, she'd been contemplating the kiss since dinner — but at the very last second her nerve had failed, that's all. "You're allowed," Kelly said. "He's not."

She has only one message — a brief note from Kelly, two days old, reinforcing her advice. She doesn't send a reply. Instead, she clicks on *New message* and types out the address she transcribed from her hand on Friday night.

Dear Alec.

No. She replaces *Dear* with *Hi*.

Hi Alec. Sorry I haven't been in touch before. An old family friend died on Saturday and I've been busy comforting his kids. He was a funny old man. He had a glass eye he used to scare me with when I was a kid. I'll miss him. Just thought I'd drop you a line to tell you how much I enjoyed dinner on Friday and to say thanks again. Drop me a line sometime. Sue.

She reads the note several times before deciding it's satisfactory — slightly chatty, personal, apparently off-the-cuff. She clicks on *Send immediately* and watches the blue bar surge briefly at the bottom of the screen. She pictures the message from Suetoo announcing itself on his screen, pictures him reading it, but is unable to imagine his reaction. In fact, it occurs to her, there isn't anything in her message for him to react to — it's so neutral — and she wonders whether she should have been a bit provoca-tive, maybe by adding a few Xs and Os before her name.

How long will it take him to reply? She remains seated before the computer for a few minutes, just in case. Two messages come in, one announcing that she has won $125,000,000 US in a lottery in Spain, the other from the widow of President Kwame Norobotu of the People's Democratic Republic of Kwanzaland, who needs her help to recoup the $80,000,000 US her husband stashed away in Switzerland before he was killed in a coup. She offers Sumintra a fifty-fifty split once the funds are safely recovered.

Sue presses the delete button twice and decides to have a cup of tea.

Seated at the kitchen table, she opens up the newspaper and runs through the help-wanted ads. They haven't changed since the weekend. Kelly mentioned some time ago that something short-term might be coming up at her office, and the temp agency where she registered promises something soon, but so far all these possibilities of something have produced nothing. Her father has mentioned, as if in passing, an ad he saw for a travel agent's course, which led her mother to wonder aloud how one became an air hostess. Her Bachelor's degree, framed and hanging on the living-room wall, no longer seems magical to them.

She throws the last of the tea into the sink and fetches the novel from her bedroom. Things aren't going well for the characters. In fact, despite all their effort, their lives are falling apart, undone by a city so chaotic that it loses people like a sieve losing water. She suspects they will all come to bad ends. That apprehension about the ugliness of their fate prompts her to want to get to the end as fast as she can. She has thought about putting it aside, but that would be against her principles, and as difficult as averting her eyes from an accident scene.

Before leaving for the park — she will sit on her favourite bench in a cool grove of trees beside the tennis courts and read — she checks her email.

Sorry, you don't have any new mail.

IT'S A QUIET morning in the park. The heat, unusual for this time of year, has scrubbed the grass of its lustre. A few kids are squabbling over a ball in the drained wading pool, their mothers or nannies perched on the concrete edge fanning themselves with hats.

She leaves them behind and enters the shady wood-chip path that leads through the stand of trees. Her bench is at the other end, just before the path gives way to the fenced-in tennis courts. Only one court is occupied, two portly women are inexpertly lobbing tennis balls at each other.

She slips her feet free of her running shoes, folds her legs beneath her on the wooden seat and opens the book. It's cooler here, the leaves are holding back the sun, but as she picks up the threads of the story, the air grows subtly oppressive, the glare on the tennis courts turns white. This morning, the radio predicted a record high and issued the usual warning to people with heart and respiratory problems. Even here in the shade, sweat beads begin oozing from her pores.

Sometime later, the tennis players, red-faced and rolling cool water bottles on their necks, stroll past her with their tennis bags.

She isn't sure how long after the women leave that the man first walks by. Engrossed in the book, reading so quickly she is almost skimming the words, she's only vaguely aware of his passage — a flash of cream trousers heading for the courts. Some minutes later he walks by again, going in the opposite direction. When she catches the flash of cream trousers for the third time, her eyes flicker up from the page at the last instant and she glimpses the back of a green T-shirt and cream cotton trousers stepping from shadow and disappearing into light. She turns back to the characters' tribulations but her concentration is eroded, a small part of her mind alert to the man's return.

And when, eventually, the man does return, that part of her mind takes over.

At first, her eyes alone rise from the page: a baseball cap with the brim tugged low, a plain green T-shirt with a patch of sweat on the chest and — this is when she raises her head, too, her mind going blank with momentary incomprehension — the crotch of his trousers ballooned by an erection.

He slows his pace, pauses and turns slightly towards her as if to ensure she has no doubt as to what she is seeing. Then, after a few leisurely steps, he breaks into a trot and within seconds is gone.

Although she knows what she has seen, she remains baffled, her mind inert. By the time she unfolds her legs, sticks her feet into her running shoes and trots after him, he is nowhere to be seen. The wading pool is deserted, there are no other witnesses. She goes back to the bench, her mind full of questions. Should she return home and call the police? But what can she tell them? That she's seen a man who had an erection *in* his pants? Can she prove that his exhibitionism was deliberate? Might it not be a matter of unfortunate timing? These things rise so easily, at such inconvenient moments. But he walked past her three times, willing her to notice him — or so it seems to her. Maybe he was just trying to walk it off? Can such a thing be walked off?

She remains on the bench for a while, seeing again the image of the ballooned crotch, reviewing the choreography of the encounter. No doubt: the display was deliberate. But the more she runs it through her mind, the more she thinks he looked less obscene than absurd, even funny in a way. And if he were an exhibitionist, hasn't she read somewhere that exhibitionists aren't rapists, they get a charge just from showing themselves?

She tries reading some more but it's no use. The characters are rocking back and forth at the edge of a precipice and she's growing impatient with the author who won't shove them off and get it over and done with. Moreover, she has declawed the man and now, unbidden, he is turning into an object of idle speculation. He is beginning to acquire features, a personality, and she is beginning to spin a narrative that begins when she smiles at him as he pauses.

She laces up her shoes and walks past the wading pool back to the house.

It is just after midday when she lets herself in. She is a little hungry, a little thirsty, but that can wait. The man in the baseball cap and green T-shirt has become Alec. He has stumbled upon her by accident and has been overtaken by his passion. He runs off because he is embarrassed by the reaction he cannot hide — but she catches up with him just beyond the wading pool, reassures him with a smile, takes him by the hand and leads him to a hidden spot among the trees.

She doesn't bother to shut her bedroom door, her need suddenly urgent. She digs the vibrator out of the drawer with one hand, with the other undoes her shorts. She is still wearing her running shoes when she lets herself fall onto the bed. With a twist of her fingers, the humming begins, the exploring. She knows that when she unzips him, she must slow down or it will all be over too fast. She tries to control the rhythm of her hand, but the thing won't let her. It is responding to her needs faster than she wishes it to.

Afterwards, she sits at the computer to check her email. Her body feels febrile, her skin prickly, and she notices that her fingers are trembling lightly as they hover over the keyboard.

You have new mail!

———

THIS IS WHAT I wrote: *The world is full of temptations and you are one of mine. Do I give in or do I turn away? Do I have a choice?*

Her reply was succinct:

I am finding you in my daydreams.

Not in her dreams, but in her daydreams. Her fantasies. Transported, I typed a quick reply asking for details — how far did those daydreams go? — but I hesitated to send it. Already, unease was beginning to seep through the adrenaline thrill. Where would this lead? I stared long and hard at the *Send immediately* bar, my fingertip nudging at the mouse. I was like a married man half-seduced by another woman: part of my instinct urging me on, another part urging caution, reminding me to understand what was at stake. The married man risks his marriage. I, on the other hand, risked a carefully tended reputation and, with it, a good part of my business. Surely it's easier to find a new wife than to rebuild a shattered reputation.

I clicked: *Send immediately*.

I'd built a career through discretion and measured manipulation of the way the world saw me. There was no reason I wouldn't be able to manage Sue in the same way.

I see now that it was a kind of arrogance.

Her reply arrived later that night. She spoke of a park, of some woods, of a hidden spot among the trees. She left nothing to the imagination.

———

KELLY SAYS, "SO when am I going to meet your mystery man?"

"Don't count on it anytime soon." Through the apartment window, pieces of sky and lake glimmer dark among the downtown buildings. The setting sun has set the summit of the golden bank tower ablaze. "He's really busy — summer's his busiest time. Besides, he's kind of shy. I don't think he's ready, which suits me just fine."

"Your folks?" Kelly bustles around the table in the small dining room beside the kitchen. She is setting out table mats and cutlery. The osso bucco is almost ready.

"They'd die if they knew. They stage-managed another accidental meeting last week. Some people they know from the temple just happened to drop by after dinner, and guess what, their unmarried pharmacist son just happened to be with them. Not bad-looking, but he hardly said a word, too busy checking out the merchandise with his eyes. I swear he had x-ray vision."

"Come on, Sue. Most guys do." She puts two wineglasses and a bottle of Italian red on the table. Sumintra picks up the bottle and uncorks it with the corkscrew that Kelly has tossed to her from the kitchen.

"Our parents were sitting right there, Kel. He was shameless."

"Not like your Alec, eh? Seems to me he could use a little bit of shamelessness."

It's been two weeks since their exchange of emails and they've seen each other twice. Both times, he's picked her up here, outside Kelly's apartment building, taken her to dinner in some out-of-the-way place, driven her back. He finds these restaurants, he says, during his weekend drives around the countryside. He claims to enjoy being alone, simply taking off on his own and forgetting about his cares. She concludes from this that he is lonely but will not admit to it. It occurs to her that the same thing could be said about her.

"He's getting there." She fills the wineglasses, takes a sip.

He hasn't said much about himself, and when she asked why he'd removed his earring, he appeared nonplussed at first and then said that he's grown tired of it. He hasn't mentioned the email she sent, and now regrets describing in detail the fantasy provoked by the man in the park. If the three-day delay was Kelly's idea of revenge, the email was hers — a little shock to his system.

Kelly serves two bowls of the fragrant osso bucco. "And how about you? You getting there?"

"I'd say so." After the second date, she accepted his lips. After the third, his tongue.

They sit across from each other and dig in. Through the window, the light thickens and the buildings acquire a stolidity that will turn magical as the sky darkens into night and their lights begin to sparkle.

"Have you told him about your parents?"

"It's a little too early for that."

"Don't wait too long. What about them? You planning on telling them about him?"

"Too early for that too. Who knows if this is going anywhere? And then there's the whole problem of his —

you know — his colour. I don't want to cause them any grief. What they don't know won't hurt them, right?"

Kelly squints at her above the rim of her wineglass. "It's hard to imagine what it's like, you know, Sue. I mean, here you are, my best friend and all, hardly any different from me, and you've got these parents who seem positively medieval."

"That's stretching it. They're not that bad. I mean, they don't walk around spewing scripture at me or anything. It's just that they've got these expectations, especially as far as my personal life goes. They think they know what'll make me happy."

"Couldn't they just buy you a car or something and leave it at that? I don't know how you put up with it."

"You get used to it, believe me. And, with the help of your friends, you find ways of getting around it as much as you can." She sucks the marrow from a chunk of bone, holds it up and spies Kelly through the hole. "Thanks, Kel."

Kelly laughs. "You're welcome. Anything I can do, let me know."

"You're already doing tons. Letting me stay here, for instance."

The agency has found her a temporary position as a fact-checker at a magazine. The hours are long, the pay modest, the offices downtown. She would waste a great deal of time on public transit and since her father cannot spare the time to drive her to and from work — his clients are mostly at construction sites in the ever-expanding suburbs — it wasn't difficult to convince them that she should accept Kelly's offer to put her up. They sent along a large can of English chocolates in thanks. She has promised to call them every evening and will return home on weekends.

"No big deal," Kelly says.

"If I get in the way —"

"I'll give you a solid kick in the butt, promise. Besides, as you see, I'm hardly ever here."

Kelly has always been one to work long and party late. In the five days since Sue's been crashing on her couch, this is the first evening they've had dinner together. Kelly has either called to say she wouldn't be in till late or she's bustled in, showered and bustled back out for an evening on the town with her boyfriend.

Sue says, "That explains the plants."

The potted plants clustered like a chunk of tropical jungle in one corner of the living room were limp and fading when Sue arrived. She has watered and fertilized them back to green lushness.

Swallowing, Kelly says, "I like having you around. I'm able to keep an eye on you. This is deep into new territory for you, Sue. It's kind of fun to watch."

A spectacle. Her life is becoming a spectacle, as amusing to Kelly as Kelly's has long been to her.

Kelly puts down her glass, sits back in the chair and lays

her palms on the table. "What is it you're looking for, Sue?"

Looking for? As far as she's aware, she's not looking for anything. She knows she isn't without ambition, but the nature of that ambition eludes her. "When I was a kid, I wanted to be a stewardess — they don't even call them that anymore, do they — and a guide at the UN and a ballerina and an actress."

"We all did, except maybe the UN thing, that's a weird one." Kelly grins, picks up her knife, taps absent-mindedly at the edge of her plate with it. "But what about when you grew up? What about now?"

Sue shrugs. Kelly won't let her dance around the truth — and she doesn't want to put that truth into words, it will sound so foolish. Architecture, English literature, the degree hanging on the wall of her parents' house: nothing ever shook the sense that she was filling time, waiting for the day when something — *the* thing — would fall into her lap and shape her days, her weeks, her years, her formless life. "You know, Kel, a boat adrift always ends up on some shore."

"Or at the bottom of the sea," Kelly says, her knife continuing to mark time on the edge of her plate.

"Well, aren't you the optimist today." Is it that she's aware of too many people whose pursuit of dreams proved pointless? That seems too simplistic — and too absurd, almost insulting, as an explanation. But she has no other. If only to stop the rhythmic rap of Kelly's knife, she says, "I'm looking for a place where I can be myself, just myself, all the time."

The tapping stops. Kelly puts down the knife, picks up her wineglass. "Choose well, Sue. Or, at least, choose carefully."

Outside, the sun's afterglow leaves the sky a greyish white, the buildings glittering silhouettes against it. "I've been careful all my life. Way I see it, a little carelessness can't hurt. It might even be called for."

After a moment, Kelly says, "I'm glad you're here, Sue. I *am* going to need to keep an eye on you."

Sue knows Kelly means well. She offers a thin smile in an approximation of gratitude. But behind the smile she thinks: Yet another pair of eyes. That makes three.

———

THE TIME WAS approaching when we would need to find some place more intimate than my leased car or a discreet table in some out-of-the-way restaurant. I didn't want her to know where I lived, and she made no move to invite me up to her apartment — her roommate seemed to be welded into the place. A hotel room was out of the question. She'd have wanted to know why we simply didn't go to my place. She'd have suspected a wife or a live-in girlfriend, demanded an explanation.

I would never have taken her to my house if she hadn't told me about her parents. Towards the end of dinner in a gloomy restaurant run by a pair of moustachioed brothers who'd fled Budapest in '56, she drained her glass of potent Hungarian red, leaned across the table and said she had something to tell me.

Secure in the knowledge she couldn't be pregnant, I poured the last of the wine into our glasses and said, "Shoot."

In a voice lightly slurred either by a touch too much wine or what she was about to tell me, she said, "Alec, I think we're going to have to end this."

My insides froze. I waited for her to go on.

"You see, I used to have an older sister."

"Used to?"

Staring into the dark ruby wine in her glass, she told me about the older sister she hardly remembered who'd been killed in an airplane explosion off the coast of Ireland. Her body had never been found.

I vaguely remembered the story, a few dozen Indians killed, something about Japan. Had the plane come from there? It was a long time ago. I made the right noises, though: how sorry I was, how awful it must have been.

"Actually," she said, "it was awful mostly for my parents. I was too young. It only became awful for me later on, thanks to them."

I asked what she meant.

"A few months after she died," she said, "they changed

my name to hers, legally." She sipped at her wine, her eyes converging on the glass. "They took away my name, the one they gave me when I was born, and gave me hers."

I must have been silent for a good minute, absorbing what she'd said. "That's horrible, Sue. Oh Christ! I shouldn't ... you must hate that name. What's your real name?"

"That *is* my real name. I grew up with it. Why would I hate it?"

"I just thought —"

"I know."

"And your parents? How do you feel about —"

"They're fine. They're good parents."

"You get along?"

"Really well."

"So what does all this have to do with you and me?"

"Think about it, Alec. I'm all they've got left. And, in a way, I'm me and my sister. I have to live for both of us — for them, you see what I mean?"

"It sounds tough but I still don't see —"

"They expect certain things of me. I mean, I don't have an older sister who'll get married to some nice Indian guy, have a bunch of kids and look after them when they get old."

"Why does it have to be an Indian guy? You don't live in India."

"*I* don't."

"So what you're saying is, they mustn't know about us."

"Which is why it's probably best if we call it quits, before things get out of hand."

"What do you mean by out of hand? We've had dinner three times, kissed a bit. That's hardly a roller coaster. Or is this just a unique way of telling me to buzz off because your folks are racist?"

"They're not racist."

"Except that if I had black skin —"

"You'd be even more unacceptable. My parents think of us as brown, café au lait as someone once called me. They expect me to marry another café au lait guy."

"Café au lait. It suits you. You're kind of like a double-double."

That brought a laugh, but she quickly became serious again. "Don't you see, Alec?" There was little conviction in her voice.

"Of course, I see." I leaned forward into the candlelight. "Do you always do that? Shut doors because the road outside might or might not lead to a cliff?" I pulled away from the light, folded my hands on my lap. "I thought you were someone else."

She smiled, twin candle flames flickering in her pupils. "I prefer streets that are dark and deserted," she said. "Is that all right with you?"

I don't know who was manipulating whom at that moment, but I do know that when we left the restaurant a few minutes later it was hand in hand. In our need for secrecy, in the way we shared with each other only those parts of our lives we judged safe to share, Sue and I were kindred spirits — or perhaps, from another perspective, we were partners in crime.

Without bothering to ask, I followed a circuitous route through dimly lit streets to my house. I parked out front. Treading softly on leaves that had fallen from the half-denuded trees, she followed me through the cool night into the darkened house.

I TURNED ON a single table lamp in the living room. More light, I felt, would have spooked her. She walked around slowly, examining the leather furnishings, peering without comment at the prints on the walls, pausing at the stack of car magazines on the coffee table. I held my breath — the mailing labels were still stuck to the magazine covers — but she moved on, drawn to an Indian batik a customer had found not to her liking.

"Nice," she said, tapping a finger at the stylized dancer behind protective glass.

"Got it for five bucks at a garage sale," I lied. "The frame alone's worth more."

Unexpectedly she said, "Can I see the car you're working on?"

"It's not ready. I'll show it to you when it's up and

running." She was being a little nosy and I hadn't prepared the house for her presence. I am a neat person. I file bills away, throw out old papers, store documents in filing cabinets, but I couldn't be absolutely certain that no other evidence of my name and my business was lying around. Pointing at the framed Central-American bark-painting beside it, I said, "What d'you think of that?"

While she was examining it, I stepped quickly into my home office, picked up a sheet of paper from the desk. She was frowning at the painting when I handed the sheet to her. "Remember this?"

She held it up to the light and bit her lower lip when she saw what it was. She tried giving it back but I insisted that she read it, aloud. She shrugged, reticent, and so, glancing down at the page still held in her hand, I began to read.

You stretch out on the grass beneath the spreading willow and I sit beside you. Your arms reach out for me but I push you back. No. You will get only what I give you. I unbutton my blouse and show you my breasts. Your eyes widen as I take them in my hands and squeeze them, rolling the stiff nipples between my fingers. Your mouth opens. I lean over you, run my nipple along your lips. You want to suck? Here, suck. My hand slides down your chest, past your belly, to the bulge in your crotch. I find the zipper, slowly draw it down …

Then she took over, her voice trembling lightly. As she read, her tongue giving new life to the words I'd so often read to myself, I observed her, eyes intense on the page, skin tight against her cheek, lips infusing the sounds with a moistness not suspected on the screen.

When she was done, she took a harsh breath and closed her eyes. I gently tugged the sheet from her hands. "I know it wasn't a promise, Sue. I know it's just fantasy from a rich imagination. You shouldn't be embarrassed."

"I'm not embarrassed." She turned her head towards me and opened her eyes. She saw me standing there beside her, my forehead slick, the front of my slacks distended. As her gaze focused on the effect her reading had had on me, her eyelids fluttered as rapidly as the wings of a bee hovering above a flower.

AFTERWARDS, SHE SAID, laughing, "You know, when I first saw you I wondered if you were gay." We were lying in my bed, in darkness just softened by the light in the corridor.

I forced a laugh. "And when I first saw you, it never crossed my mind that you were a virgin."

"I was not!" she said.

"Could've fooled me."

She'd been nervous when we began, her eagerness a little forced. She had handled me roughly and I'd had to loosen her grip, slow down her rhythm. Her inexperience was obvious. She seemed relieved when I pushed her gently onto her back and whispered to her to lie still. My journey down her body — pausing at a soft breast, at a stiffened nipple, tracing her rib cage with my lips, her hips with my hands — elicited a series of sighs and grunts and whimpers. My head slid between her legs and her body arched, lifting her hips, her hands grasping the back of my head to pull me so tightly against that moist and pungent warmth that I could hardly breathe. Was the trembling that seized her body a sign of the approaching storm? Or was it — a curious impression: she was like someone terrified of what she most wanted at that moment — a fear of that storm? Her climax was long and powerful and left us both gasping for breath.

When, a few minutes later, I entered her, I was only half-surprised to meet a little resistance. I pushed, she twitched once as if stung, and the resistance gave way. Fired up by her intensity, rocked by the rhythms of a peculiar poetry she breathed into my ear, my own climax was not long in coming.

"I was only half a virgin," she whispered playfully, pressing herself to my side and laying her palm on my chest.

"Meaning?"

"You're the first guy I've been with."

"So, was it a woman?"

"God no, that doesn't interest me."

"What then?"

"That's my little secret."

I let it drop. I would respect her secrets, big and small. I would expect the same in return.

———

SEATED WITH KELLY at an outdoor table of the new Tex-Mex restaurant, Sue tugs her sweater more firmly about her shoulders. She has been bothered by the lie she told Alec, turning the other Sumintra into an older sister. She doesn't know why she did this — it just slipped from her tongue. Nor can she fathom why it should bother her. She just knows that it does. The sun is going down earlier now and the great heat of summer has mostly given way to the cooler air of fall. On the sidewalk, sweaters and windbreakers jostle with T-shirts and tank tops.

Working a cheese-smothered nacho free from the large plate in front of them, Kelly says, "So what are you going to do about Alec?" She scoops up some guacamole and balances a ring of hot pepper on it. "Your parents'll be expecting you to move back home soon."

Sue takes a sip of the sangria that Kelly has poured from a glazed earthenware jug. Next Friday, the temporary job will draw to an end and the agency tells her that, for the moment, nothing else is available.

Kelly wipes her fingertips on a napkin. "Seems to me you've got two choices. Tell your folks or end it. There's no avoiding it, unless you can find some way to sneak around. You know, Sue, I don't care what time you come

THE SOUL OF ALL GREAT DESIGNS

in or where you've been or what you've been up to — so long as you come in and you look happily worn out. But your parents, that's another story. One way or another somebody's going to get hurt, you for sure and whoever loses the lottery."

Kelly has probed a bit about Alec, but Sue has kept her answers vague. He thinks it best, and she agrees, that their worlds be kept utterly separate. There is nothing to be gained from his meeting her roommate — she recognizes that they are such different people, Alec and Kelly — and it would be a useless breach of the discretion they have been so careful to cultivate. So she has told Kelly that he is a house painter, that he does well enough to own a nice house in a quiet neighbourhood, that he is a good house-keeper with good taste, and that he is an attentive lover, gentle most of the time, rough only when she wants him to be. They have been spending a lot of time together, she and Alec. She knows her answers don't really satisfy Kelly — there isn't enough nitty-gritty and what she says makes Alec appear a little bland — but Alec has been so mindful of her desire for covertness that she can't bring herself to betray his consideration, not even to her best friend.

What she cannot tell Kelly is that the power of this thing called *desire* staggers her. Even the word doesn't seem robust enough: the right word should have jagged edges, with Js and Vs and Zs that would scald the lips that shaped it and the ear that heard it. Maybe the word doesn't exist, she thinks, the one word that would encapsulate the kind of madness — invasive, obsessive, irresistible in its possession of her — that imposes another personality. Maybe it is the search for this word that causes her to chorus into Alec's ear a stream of four-letter words, every one she can think of — words that have coursed forever through her mind and which she can only now release safely. They come of their own volition, the words, in a voice not her own, emerging from deep in her flesh. She doesn't know what Alec thinks of the words, what effect they have on him: she is so engulfed in the maelstrom, she is hardly aware of him as Alec, is aware only of his weight, his warmth, his vigour inside her. Afterwards, she is astonished that the tongue that emits those words can still say *Mamu* and *Papu* and maintain an intelligent conversation. She finds it unsettling that all those words reside in the same place, that they are all equally part of her.

Two of Kelly's fingers dip into her glass of sangria and emerge with an ice cube. Her hands slide beneath the table. When they re-emerge, they are curled into fists. She stretches her arms above the plate of nachos towards Sue. "Ice cube, you keep him and you tell your parents. No ice cube, you get rid of him and your parents are none the wiser."

"Don't be silly, Kelly."

"Don't take too long, the darn thing's cold."

"I'm not going to choose."

"You have to. This is as good a way as any."

For the first time, Sue feels she's being pushed by Kelly down a path she doesn't want to take. Resentment tightens her chest, her breathing goes shallow. She wants to tell her to fuck off. Still, Kelly's small fists are aimed at her, the knuckles pushing whitish through her fading tan, daring her. It's like *eenie-meenie-minie-moe*. A game: the choice commits her to nothing. If she had to choose, which one would she ...?

A drop of water falls from Kelly's right fist and lands on the tablecloth.

"The right," Sue says.

Kelly opens her palm, the melting ice cube in the middle of her reddened palm. "You can't fool me, Sue. Any longer and my hand would've been like a leaky tap."

Sue stares at the ice cube, watches it slide from Kelly's palm and alight on the tablecloth, engulfing the drop that gave the game away. But now that the choice is made, it no longer feels like a game. It feels like a decision.

She is startled when Kelly's cold hand grabs her forearm. She looks up into eyes widened in alarm, the blue irises crystalline and brittle.

"Fuck, Sue," Kelly says. "You're not falling in love with him, are you?"

———

THAT YEAR, FALL roared in on glacial winds. Cottages were long closed and shuttered, and people had returned to work. Business picked up, renovation and redecoration jobs to be completed before Christmas. I became less available for Sue — I was working long hours, six, sometimes seven days a week. I would return home exhausted and there were even times when I crashed in the storeroom at work. The espresso machine was constantly on the go. I'd finished the restoration of the Chevy, but there was no time to enjoy it. If I could, I would take it out before the first snow. If not, it would have to wait until spring.

As luck would have it, Sue became less available for me, too. In an email, she mentioned some new project at work that required all her time and attention. We managed to see each other only twice in three weeks, a quick bite followed by languorous sex. I can't say I'd missed her, but I was happy to see her wrapped in a thick royal blue cape waiting for me at the door of the apartment building. Both times she had to wake me afterwards so I could drive her back to her place.

Sue and I filled comfortable niches for each other. There was never a question of our going out on the town — no cinemas or theatres or concerts, no nursing drinks in noisy bars or performing sweaty contortions on dance floors. If even the friend of a friend of a friend of her parents were to spot us, word would get back. Their community, she said, was that tight. We did engage in some idle talk about getting away for a weekend to some place far enough to be safe, but she feared that if she were out of touch for an entire weekend, her parents would report her missing. But couldn't her roommate cover for her? Only for a few hours, she said. They would expect her to call the moment she got in, at whatever hour. So we spent evenings together always in the shadows — the interior equivalent of those darkened, deserted streets she once mentioned.

I couldn't have asked for more.

And then, late one evening when I got home from the office, I found an email from her. The following weekend, from early Friday afternoon to late Sunday night, her parents would be out of town. They were religious types and their temple, as she called it, had rented a summer camp's deserted facilities for a weekend retreat in the country. They would be relaxing and meditating and reading scriptures — and, best of all, there would be no telephones. Even cellphones were banned. A perfect weekend, she wrote, for our own little retreat.

Except that I had to work, shuttling between two projects — a kitchen renovation and a basement refurbishing — whose contracts had promised completion for the Sunday evening. Nothing had ever come between me and my work, although at this point my involvement was less hands-on than planning and quality control.

I tapped out a quick response explaining the situation and apologizing profusely. But I couldn't bring myself to send it. Throughout my long hot shower, recent memories kept nagging at me: the warmth of her back on my palm, how her hair curtained her face when she took me in her mouth and how she thrust her hips at me when I took her with mine, the grasp of her hands on my buttocks pulling me deeper, the way she would whimper her poetry into the pillow when, my face burrowed into the nape of her neck, I entered her from behind. I emerged from the shower with a hard-on so insistent that it distracted me until I took care of it.

Towelling off, the solution occurred to me. Both jobs were being performed by experienced work teams. I would appoint the most dependable member of each team foreman — although the word wouldn't do, it was too old-fashioned, too reminiscent of street labour — and promise a healthy bonus (and why not the team members too) if the work was done on time, to specifications and with the elegant finish the company was known for.

Pleased but yawning, I deleted my email and wrote another: I would pick her up outside her apartment building at six on Friday. By the time I clicked on *Send immediately*, I had found the title I would bestow on my foremen: On-site Project Manager or OPM. There's nothing like having an acronym attached to his name to make a man take his responsibilities seriously. By the time I crawled into bed, I'd dropped the idea of bonuses for the team members. They had their jobs to do and it made no difference whether it was me or the OPM breathing down their necks.

———

HER FATHER COMES to greet her at the door when she lets herself in. "Daughter," he says, squeezing her shoulder. "Home at last."

She sees immediately that he is in a febrile state. Something's up. The house smells of food — lots of food. Her mother's been busy. In the living room, a man stands blinking rapidly at her through thick-framed glasses. His hair is greying and he is well-dressed, in a suit and tie. She figures he's in his late thirties or early forties, but it's hard to tell sometimes with Indian men.

Her father says, "Daughter, we have a guest this evening." He looks quickly over his shoulder. "I am having the honour to introduce Professor Motilal Mukherjee." He nudges her forward. "Professor Mukherjee, my daughter Sumintra."

As her father takes her coat, Sumintra fights the urge to flee, forces her legs to take her to the living room, her hand outstretched.

Professor Mukherjee grazes her palm with his, as if he's wary of grasping her hand. "Good evening, miss," he says with a nervous smile.

"Hi," Sumintra says. "Glad to meet you." He is a small man, neat, with a mole low down on his left cheek. He smells of talcum powder even through her mother's spices. His suit looks second-hand, or at least well-worn, but so did the clothes of most of her former university professors. That reassures her: he doesn't look like the usual man invited to play a cameo in her life with an eye to a leading role.

Her father says, "We were just talking about you."

"Were you?" She should have smiled, she thinks, but it's too late now. Perhaps her parents are willing to put anyone on offer, so long as he has a degree or two hanging on some wall and a steady job.

"I'll go give Mamu a hand in the kitchen," Sumintra says. And for the second time in as many minutes, she rebukes herself: now he'll think she can cook, perfect marriage material.

"Yes, yes, you do that," her father says. "I was just about to get us some drinks. We can all talk at dinner."

"Great," she says. "I'll have a scotch."

"But ... but you don't drink, daughter."

At the kitchen door, she glances back at him. The pleading desperation in his eyes confirms her fears.

AT DINNER — HER parents have set the formal dining table, complete with cutlery and the good water glasses — her mother seats her across from Professor Mukherjee. His neatness, she sees, extends to his table manners. He doesn't so much grasp his knife and fork as hold them gingerly in the tips of his fingers. The passage of food from his plate to his mouth is affected with care, deliberation, as if to ensure that not a grain of rice will fling itself to safety.

During the halting conversation led by her father, whose manner brings to mind that of an anxious interviewer, she learns that he is employed at a nuclear research institute but that he is not free to divulge the nature of his job. "My work is very hush-hush," he says. "Highest security clearance. I had to acquire special permission from our security authorities to make this trip."

Sumintra says, "So what brings you here?"

He smiles wanly at his plate. "That too is hush-hush."

Her father says, "Please do not put Professor Mukherjee in a tight spot, daughter. We must be more discreet."

Great, Sumintra thinks, reaching for her water glass. A spy. James Bond without the looks. She turns towards her father. "So how do you know each other, Papu?"

"Professor Mukherjee's father was my mentor at the engineering firm back home, daughter. He was the senior man in my section. He took me under his wing, showed me the ropes, advised me. He was very disappointed when we decided to emigrate. The professor tells me he is not in good health."

"Sorry to hear that," Sumintra says, with a glance at Professor Mukherjee.

"My father is no longer a young man," he says, patting at his lips with his napkin. "Your sentiment is kind but unnecessary."

She feels like apologizing — *Sorry I said I'm sorry your dad's sick, forgive me, you prick* — but she is saved from making an awkward moment even more so by her mother's offer of more water.

Her father says, "Professor Mukherjee was the water boy for the company's cricket team. He did a bang up job! Tell me, did you ever take up cricket yourself?"

"Too vigorous for me, I'm afraid, all that running — not good for the knees."

As dinner proceeds, Sumintra learns that Professor Mukherjee is a widower, that his wife died from complications in childbirth and that his daughter is being brought up by his sister. "She is nine or ten now," he says. "She does very well at school."

"And does your sister have children of her own?" her mother says.

"Sadly, no," he says. "She and her husband have been blessed in other ways. But my daughter is like a daughter to her. They are very lucky."

Centring her knife and fork on her plate which is devoid of all but an excess of rice, Sumintra thinks that Professor Mukherjee is the saddest man she's ever met.

HER MOTHER THOROUGHLY scrubs and washes each plate under running hot water at the sink before passing it to Sumintra, who then places it in the dishwasher rack for its second washing. Like her preference for razor blades over electric shavers, this after-meal ritual is one of her inextinguishable habits.

Taking a plate from her, Sumintra says, "Don't you think he's a little old for me, Mamu?"

Holding a soapy plate to the water, her mother says, "What do you mean, daughter?"

"He must be almost twice my age. Besides, with his job and his security clearance, he's not likely to want to move here, is he? Give it up, Mamu. You and Papu aren't the most subtle people in the world. Professor Mukherjee's in the market and you're showing me off like some kind of fresh vegetable."

Her mother's fingers grip so tightly at the plate, her arms shake. "Sumintra! I will not have you talking like that."

"I'm tired of it, Mamu. The engineers and the pharmacists and the nuclear physicists. And I can't believe you'd want me to go off and live in India with this man!"

"Keep your voice down!" says her mother in a furious whisper.

"Why should I?"

Her mother leans in close. "Don't mess this one up, Sumintra! You are running out of choices."

Sumintra is about to reply — *Not me*, she will say. *You're the one who's running out of choices* — when a look of bewilderment materializes on her mother's face. She follows her gaze downwards and sees that the plate her mother has been holding has snapped silently in two.

———

I AM IN what appears to be the living room of an old but beautifully maintained apartment — terrazzo floors, windowsills and baseboards of dark woodwork, simple white walls, sparse furnishings: a red armchair, the shadow of a small cabinet in one corner. Through the large, open window, I see that the sky is grey and cloudy, the air full of mist and fog, and that just outside large ships are ploughing through the widened mouth of a river to the ocean which I know to be nearby. To my left, across from the window, an arched doorway leads to the kitchen: counters, a white granite sink beneath opaque windows, the floor covered in a fine and complicated mosaic of miniscule green and mustard tiles. I know somehow that the apartment is irregularly shaped. With me in the living room is a man I cannot identify but whom I know, in the dream. He is tall, wiry, with curly black hair cut short, and is wearing a long-sleeved maroon shirt and black trousers. He lives in the apartment and, in response to my question, tells me how he came to rent it: the previous tenant had to flee, he took it off her hands. It is time for me to leave. Pulling on a shirt — I haven't noticed until now that I have been shirtless — I turn towards an oval, gilt-framed mirror hanging on the wall behind me and begin doing up the buttons. Through the corner of my eye, I see the man's face freeze in dismay — and at that very moment I see, in the mirror, that there is a strange growth on my left arm: three horizontal strips of flesh each the width of a belt and the colour of wet coffee grounds, the ends dangling loose. More in curiosity than anything else, I raise my right hand to feel the detached end of one of the growths — it is like soft rubber — only to have my attention jerked towards another growth: a fully developed hand, a replica of my own right hand, open palm facing outwards, growing just above my heart. With dismay, with embarrassment, with repulsion and a light nausea, I wonder how it is I've never seen these things before, how it is that the ladies from the agency, faced with such ugliness, were still able to perform their duties. Quickly buttoning my shirt to the neck, I think I will have to see a doctor to get them excised.

SHE SMELLED OF lavender when I picked her up at the apartment building.

Buckling her seat belt, she said, "You look tired." Her eyes were bright, her gestures skittish. She was on edge.

The emerald green of her blouse wasn't quite her colour. She placed a small overnight bag at her feet.

"It's a busy time."

"You need some TLC," she said as I pulled out into the traffic. We didn't kiss: that was for the shadows.

Her words irritated me. I hadn't stocked up on food and wine and condoms because I was looking forward to tender loving care. My interests were far more carnal than that. "No need to worry about me, I'll be fine."

"I'm going to wear you out this weekend."

"We'll see who wears who out," I said, soothed by the promise and heartened by the hand slipping between my thighs.

ROLLING THUNDER WOKE me the next morning, the third bang followed by the crash of heavy rain. Wind stirred the drapes. I rolled out of bed to shut the window, noticing at the same time that Sue wasn't there. Outside, brown leaves were being ripped from their branches.

I found her in the kitchen wearing one of my white shirts. Her back was to me, and she was standing barefoot at the counter cracking eggs into a bowl. Beside the egg carton were tomatoes, a cucumber and a loaf of bread. She had found the cutting board, the knives, the frying pan, the salt and pepper. In the corner beside the stove, the coffee machine gurgled and steamed. Beyond the window in front of her, rain from the angry sky whipped by almost horizontally.

Leaning naked and undetected against the doorframe, I observed her for a minute. Her hair was tied back in a ragged ponytail. In my shirt, sleeves rolled to the elbows, her shoulders were squared and the curves of her hips hidden by the shirttail. Her bare feet were squarely planted on the vinyl-tiled floor. I watched her whisk the eggs vigorously, salt and pepper them, whisk them some more. She had made herself at home and that sight — of Sue domesticated — vaguely unsettled me.

She must have sensed my presence. She glanced over her shoulder at me, eyed my nakedness, lingered. "Eggs?" she said.

I came close to her.

She half-turned towards me, bowl in one hand, whisk in the other.

I said, "Take off my shirt."

She frowned, puzzled, at me.

"Take off my shirt."

"Why?"

"Just do it."

Uncertain, she put the whisk into the bowl and the bowl onto the counter. She undid the first three buttons of the shirt, pulled it off over her head and held it out to me.

I tossed it onto the kitchen table and, folding my arms across my chest, took a slow, searching look at her body, from top to bottom: the sturdy, bony shoulders; the slender arms; the small breasts, of a lighter brown halfway down, with the dark, off-centre nipples pointing slightly to the sides; the flat belly, the curved hips; the perfect black triangle of her pubic hair; the firm thighs; the knees with their rumpled skin; her small calves and shapely, high-arched feet, the nails trimmed and unpainted.

Her frown transformed itself into a look of unease. "Alec, what do you —"

"That's much better." I smiled. "Scrambled, please."

SHE WAITED UNTIL late the following afternoon to say, "Alec, I want to talk to you about something."

We were sprawled naked on the living-room carpet, out of condoms and so sore and spent neither of us felt the need to go buy more. The clouds were finally beginning to lighten and the windows admitted a thin, grey glare.

"What?" I said, propping myself up on my elbows.

She was flat on her back beside me, hands resting on her belly, eyes shut, hair in disarray. "I want you to meet my roommate, Kelly."

I was silent for a moment. She'd mentioned once that Kelly was an architect; there was a chance that our circles had overlapped. "Why?"

Her lips twitched. "Then I want you to meet my parents."

"Hold on." I sat up straight, my abdominal muscles

wrenching at the sudden movement. "What's this all about, Sue?"

"I don't want to continue like this. Kel pointed out to me I'd have to choose between you and my parents. She was right. I choose you."

Christ! *I choose you.* She looked very happy when she said those words but they fell like atonal music on my ears: without melody, without rhythm, a song played on a piano hopelessly out of tune.

"You've told your roommate about me?"

"Only your name, don't worry. When I decide to be discreet, I'm discreet."

Her understanding of discretion was more flexible than mine.

"She's curious about you, though. It'll be tough with my parents, but at least Kelly'll be there for us. That's something, don't you think?"

"Sue, do you think it's a good idea, coming out?"

"It's what I want, Alec. I've forced you to live like a criminal and you've been great about it. But it's time I faced up to things." She snickered. "I want to make an honest man out of you."

It was then that the truth reeled into my head: she had fallen in love with me, of all things. I said, "I'm happy the way things are. I mean, how are your parents going to react? I might never see you again."

She opened her eyes, blinked at me. "Understand, Alec, it's not *you* that I wouldn't be seeing again." She eased herself up and slung her arms around my neck. When she kissed me, I had no choice but to kiss her back.

WE WERE WAITING for Chinese takeout, the lights turned low, Bill Evans tinkling in the background, when she said, "There's something mysterious about you, Alec. Something I can't put my finger on." We'd showered, dressed, poured ourselves some white wine and settled into the sofa, her head in my lap.

I took a sip of my wine, then another, and carefully set the glass on the side table. With the remote, I turned the music up a little. Finally, I said, "So much the better. A little mystery's good. Keeps the interest up, don't you think?"

She turned her face away, shrugged — but the gesture, hardly more than a ripple of her shoulders, was unconvincing. She wanted more, wanted a glimpse at the mystery, and her curiosity was causing her to tiptoe into territory on which Caroline had once infringed. She would not get far. I drew her attention to a painting I'd recently bought by a young artist who was attracting a great deal of attention. The few hundred dollars I'd paid for the colourful squiggles were expected to appreciate significantly in the coming years. Feigning enthusiasm — a valuable talent in my field — and ignoring her indifference, I took her through the particularities of the painting — the meaning of the colours individually, the meaning of the colours collectively, how a brush stroke to the left complemented and contradicted a brush stroke to the right, how the placement of the single red dot in the lower right-hand corner both induced the concept of ethnicity and sub-verted it, etcetera, etcetera — just as they'd been pointed out to me *ad nauseum* by the gallery owner, a good client of mine.

She listened without interruption but, evidently, with a single ear.

For the first time, surely without knowing it, Sue was experiencing my professional self.

People like me — and almost everyone's like me, although hardly anyone wants to acknowledge it — come to inhabit our roles completely. We *are* our roles. Wasn't it Shakespeare who wrote *All the world's a stage and all the men and women merely players*? Or something like that, high-school lit classes go back a ways. Smart guy, that Will. Psychobabble's always jabbering at us that we must strive to be real, genuine, true to ourselves. Centuries ago, Shakespeare knew that was meaningless crap. These selves of ours we're supposed to be true to are constructions — the roles we play, roles that are either given to us or that we invent ourselves. More useful advice would be: Be true to the role you're stuck with. Most people would recoil from that thought but take impulsiveness, for example.

Kids are naturally impulsive, they're born that way, yet parents spend years drumming it into them that that's a bad thing. *Think before you act.* Don't you dare jump into that mud puddle even if you're dying to. And the moment you hold back, the moment you step around the mud puddle, you're not being true to yourself. You're assuming a role and the personality that goes with it — the good little kid who shoves his true self into some dark corner.

The role I've written for myself is perhaps more complex than most. Nobody imposed it on me, after all. And I didn't simply fall into it, either. I've designed it by playing with people's stereotypes, by using their own prejudices against them and to my advantage. I never really expected things to go as far as they have. Who'd have thought that that moment of teenaged frustration leading to that frankly outrageous resolution would provoke material success and consequently shape a whole life? Who'd have thought that that moment would end up trapping me? How could I have known I'd still be playing this game so many years later?

But there it is. I am enmeshed and have become my role, like all of us.

This role is at the heart of the mystery Sue was reaching for. She wanted to know who I am. But who I am is what I've constructed — ungraspable and enigmatic, fluid even to myself — and nothing, *nothing*, is more precious to me.

When I finished my spiel of artsy babbly, Sue took a gulp of wine, stretchèd and said, "So how's the car coming along?"

"The Chevy? It's done."

"Really? When'd you find the time?"

"A bit here, a bit there. It's the only way you can do something like that."

She asked to see it and I groggily agreed. We'd tried to make love one last time and it hadn't worked. I'd pleaded fatigue, conceding that she'd won the bet as to who would wear who out — but the truth is that this new twist was eating away at me. Is there anything more nerve-racking than being without choice?

We made our way down through the basement to the garage. The fluorescent tubes flickered on and I carefully withdrew the car-cover to reveal the Chevy, its green body and black running boards glistening fresh in the light.

Sue appeared mesmerised. She stepped close to it, gingerly ran her fingertips along the hood, onto the chrome of the radiator, around the chrome and glass of the head-lights. She walked all the way around, peering inside at the reupholstered seats, putting a hand through the open window to grasp the steering wheel.

She said, "Does it work?"

"Like new. The entire engine's been cleaned, greased, new parts put in."

"Let's go for a spin," she said.

"Can't just yet. Before I can take her out on the street, she has to be inspected, certified, registered, insured. If the cops stopped us —"

"Let's go anyway."

"Sorry, that'd be a reckless thing to do."

"This entire weekend is reckless, Alec. And what's coming next, that's reckless too. I'm willing to chance it."

"Slow down, Sue. I could lose the car, not to mention my licence and god knows what else."

She leaned her back against the car and slipped the strap of her dress down her left arm, exposing her left breast. "Well," she said, "I'm in the mood for a ride, if not in it then on it."

She'd never said anything like that before. This was well beyond her promise, which now seemed almost demure, to wear me out. It recalled her email, her whispered poetry. It was a glimpse into desires which took me unawares. She was full of the unexpected that evening. I found it unsettling

She half-smiled at the stirring in my crotch. Then she gathered up the skirt of the dress, the same blue one with white moons she'd worn on our first date, and wrapped it around her waist. She wasn't wearing panties. She turned around and draped herself on the hood of the Chevy, leaving her right foot securely anchored on the ground and perching the left on the running board.

I approached her, unzipping my pants.

She was very wet. I grasped her hips and, after just a few strokes, with her right arm squeezed between her body and the hood so she could claw at herself, she came shuddering against the car, her breath fogging the green paint beneath her mouth. I withdrew at the last moment, so drained by the weekend only a few specks of clear liquid sprinkled onto her brown rump. In the distance arose the insistent barking of a house alarm.

Two days later, giving a final polish to the car, I discovered several deep scratches on the hood, probably from the bangles she'd worn on her wrist. The entire hood would have to be redone.

IN ONE OF her less physical columns, Tawny, my first receptionist who has long since moved on from the newspaper to bestselling books and a weekly sex-advice television show, once wrote that a relationship is won a little and lost a little every day. For the relationship to survive, the won column should be longer than the lost column by the end of each and every evening.

I see it slightly differently. To me, every relationship comes with a scale. My parents' was on the whole a perfect balance of contentment and dissatisfaction, just enough to keep things even. It doesn't take much to unbalance things.

I was awake for a long time after I dropped Sue off at her apartment later that night. Without knowing it, she had tipped our scale way off-kilter. I had no idea what I would do when she sent the promised email setting up a drink with her roommate.

The message came that Thursday. There really was no choice. Perhaps her roommate would help me convince her to change her mind? As for being seen in public with two women, they could be clients, couldn't they? I even prepared a cover story should her roommate recognize me. This interior-decorator guy — my cousin, a strong family resemblance, he was the big success in the family, even if he was a fairy. Can't stand the bastard though — here I was, his fucking cousin, a painter, and does he toss any work my way? Not on your fucking life. Let's change the goddamned subject ...

Another, less appealing aspect of Alec to present to Sue.

———

THE HOUSE IS empty when she lets herself in. Every Friday morning, after her father has left for his day on the road, her mother takes a series of buses across town to meet a group of women at the temple. They will spend three hours there, between nine and twelve, singing and gossiping as they sweep and wash and polish. This is her mother's way of compensating for the large financial donations others can afford but that she and her husband cannot.

The first thing she notices when she shuts the door on

the silence is the smell, traces of a complex amalgam of ghee, browned onions, burnt sugar and a handful of spices — *elaichi, jeera, mirchi*, probably *dhaniya* and *haldi* — blended into one. The aroma tells her that, before leaving, her mother spent hours in the kitchen, most likely rising before dawn to prepare a variety of dishes for a communal meal at the temple this weekend.

When Sumintra was younger, her mother had wanted to teach her how to cook their foods: samosas and pilaus and various curries, chapatis and *parathas*, the sweet *rass-gulla* and *chaler payesh* that her father — and, by extension, Sumintra's future husband — relished. The cooking classes hadn't been very successful, Sumintra silently resentful of the hovering phantom of the future father of her children. She had acquired certain basics — her *avial*, plantains, beans and carrots in a yoghurt and coconut sauce, was quite good — but she hadn't mastered the art. She had insisted on writing everything down and frustrated her mother by her need for precision. Her mother, fingers pinching at the spices, would say, "A little *haldi*, then a little *dhaniya*" and Sumintra, pen hovering over her sheet of paper, would say, "Yes, Mamu, but *how much* turmeric, *how much* coriander? A teaspoon? A tablespoon?" and her mother, with the slightest hint of exasperation, would say, "I don't know, Sumin. Maybe half a teaspoon of *haldi*, maybe half a teaspoon ... no, a teaspoon of *dhaniya*." She hadn't found it at all funny the day that Sumintra, after accidentally burning bay leaves and cumin seeds in hot oil, declared that perhaps she would just marry a cook and solve the problem. After that, her mother seemed to lose interest in passing along her culinary expertise, encouraging her instead to concen-trate on her studies. Sumintra knew, as did her mother, that the hovering phantom would want an educated wife as well, preferably a professional of some kind. Her parents were deflated when she switched from architecture — already a step down from a career in medicine or the sciences — to literature. Teachers were not hot property in the marriage market.

Sumintra moves gingerly through the living room, her soft leather bag hanging lightly from her shoulder. The drapes are drawn shut on the rainy day outside and no lights have been left on. The damp soles of her running shoes squeak on the parquet. She should have removed them at the door but she doesn't plan to be here long. As she makes her way past the kitchen, the odours grow more distinct and, for the first time, they strike her as being reminders of failure. Maybe she should have taken the cooking more seriously. Alec likes different kinds of food and, although they have avoided Indian restaurants, she's sure he would love her mother's cooking. A sadness comes to her when she thinks they are unlikely to be invited to dinner with her parents, but by the time she's at the door of her room hardly ten steps later, she has pushed the feeling away and resolved to hunt for a good Indian cookbook.

The curtains in her room are half-drawn and in the grey light she sees that her mother has been in here, dusting, neatening. *Being her mother.* A little doubt curls into Sue's belly. She pictures it as a wisp of black smoke, its presence hardly more substantial but as irrefutable. Suddenly weary, she sits on her bed and the smell of fabric softener rises from the sheets. Lavender: it gives her a pleasure she considers a touch infantile. For years, her mother has used the same scent. Does that make her predictable — in Kelly's vocabulary, almost a term of derision — or does it make her dependable, reliable, reassuring? It occurs to her that a certain degree of predictability is essential to a sense of dependability.

Rain splatters against the windowpane. The wind is picking up. Sumintra reaches for her pillow, hugs it to her chest, buries her nose in its softness. She wonders whether she is underestimating her parents. They don't seem to be quite like the others she knows. Mr. Kumar, for instance. She finds it hard to imagine that he would have her father's sense of humour or his ease of conversation. As for Mrs. Kumar and her mother, they could hardly be less alike.

The smoke in her belly begins to dissipate. Perhaps they won't be like the others in their community. Perhaps, after their initial anger and shame and disappointment, they'll adjust to Alec, learn to tolerate his presence if not quite to accept him. Who knows what magic the birth of a grand-son might work?

The thought of Mr. and Dr. Prasad gives her pause, though. Did Rima ever think, even for a second, that her thoroughly modern, professional parents would exile her over a boy? A mental picture, years old, takes shape in her mind: Rima cowering in some dark and stuffy room in a houseful of strangers somewhere in India. What would Rima look like now? she wonders. What could have happened to her intelligence, her confidence? Who, today, after all these years, would Rima be?

She takes a deep breath of her pillow, of the lavender scent. Sumintra knows that her parents love her and that she loves them. But she realizes that somewhere deep down, in some fundamental place, she does not trust them. Yes, this has to do with Rima, with Mr. and Dr. Prasad's scandalous treatment of her and with her parents' equally scandalous defence of them. But there is more. Part of the equation is their not allowing her to work summers when she was in high school and university. She feels now that she knew then, even as she enjoyed her free time, that their refusal had less to do with ensuring her a youth as carefree as theirs had been than with keeping an eye on her and making her dependent on their money: to be certain that she lived her life as they wished. And, of course, there is their gentle suspicion of Kelly. It seems to her that she has always known this instinctively but has been unable to see it with any clarity until now.

Until Alec.

It's time to move. She fluffs the pillow and replaces it with her mother's precision at the head of the bed. She knows what she wants to do and dwelling on the reasons seems almost superfluous. What took root in the mind has already moved resolutely into the flesh. She steps quickly over to her desk, pulls open the middle drawer and digs her hand through the strata of pens and pencils and erasers and other paraphernalia going back to her early years in high school. Her hand finds the velvet bag. She tosses it, along with her CD player, into her shoulder bag and shoves the drawer shut.

Her shoes no longer squeak on the floor as she strides from her bedroom, down the corridor and into her parents' darkened bedroom. The only light is from a plastic, candle-shaped lamp, the yellow bulb glows in her parents' prayer corner. She doesn't need light to find the grey, fireproof box under the bed in which her father keeps important documents. The manila envelope with her name hand-printed on it is near the bottom. She takes a quick look: her birth certificate, her vaccination record and her two passports bound together by a rubber band. She closes the box and carefully slides it back under the bed to precisely where she found it.

Before leaving the house, she hesitates only slightly before pulling the front door shut and turning the key in the lock. Twice.

Alone at the bus stop, she tosses the velvet bag into the garbage can, a gesture of faith in a reclaimed future, like an alcoholic smashing his unfinished bottles or a smoker crushing a half-full pack. Then, sitting on the narrow bench inside the shelter, she pulls the hood of her raincoat over her head, clutches the envelope on her lap and waits.

———

WE WERE TO meet at the Den, a watering hole just east of downtown that was frequented by stockbrokers and banking people on their way up but not yet at income levels that could afford my company's services. On the whole, a safe spot that had the advantage of being sunken below street level. I could park in the underground garage, take the elevator to the second floor and unobserved, before committing myself, check out the bar and tables.

Rehearsing my cover story so that there were enough details to be plausible but not so many as to lead to further conversation, I took the elevator up and emerged onto the carpeted second-floor balcony overlooking the Den. Obscured by the indoor plants hung along the railing, I peered down. It was early still, the place was half-empty. I immediately recognized Sue, even though she sat facing away from me. Across from her talking on a cellphone was her roommate. When I saw Kelly's face, my body froze, hunching involuntarily into the spurt of fern in front of me.

Kelly would recognize me just as I'd recognized her. She would recognize me as Bud from Sacramento or Pete from Pasadena or Frank from Minneapolis, just passing through on business. I couldn't think of the name she'd given herself, but she was one of those college girls who claimed to be making ends meet — not really a whore, you see, it's just that life in the big city was so expensive, she just took the occasional call, a way of tiding things over.

One thing I learned from Tawny is that women will go to extraordinary lengths to protect each other.

I pressed the elevator button. When I pulled out of the parking garage, my tires squealed.

HER EMAIL WAS full of rage, especially since Kelly was off for two weeks in the Dominican Republic and we wouldn't be able to meet until she got back. It took me a full hour to concoct a response full of contrition. I couldn't plead an emergency at work — what kind of emergency could a house painter possibly have? I claimed car trouble, a steaming engine in rush hour on the parkway. And of course, I couldn't reach her. I concluded by promising a special evening dedicated to her pleasure — a bath in lavender water, a massage with scented oils, champagne, silk sheets for the bed.

Her answer, which was several days in coming, was terse but subdued. She specified that the champagne had to be French.

I was playing for time, looking for a way out. Sue had made the situation untenable. I feared the depth of passion she'd revealed during our weekend together, the price she was willing to pay for a life with me. Simply breaking it off with her was out of the question. She knew where I lived. What was to prevent her from coming and pounding at my door, maybe even with Kelly as backup? Just imagining the possibility caused my heart to hammer and my skin to go clammy.

Somehow, I would have to convince her that bringing our relationship out of the closet was the wrong thing to do.

ONE EVENING A few days later, I kept my promise. I served her champagne in a lavender-scented bath, gave her a long, searching rubdown with massage oil, my fingers pressing with gentle vigour, yet at times — when I forgot myself — with impatience, at every centimetre of skin between her temples and her toes. My hands relaxed her in some ways, stimulated her in others. The silk sheets, disagreeable to my skin, heightened the sensitivity of hers:

she growled, each time with growing intensity, through a series of orgasms.

Afterwards, we lay beside each other finishing the champagne, the air odorous with the muskiness of massage oil, fresh sweat and lavender. "Sue," I said, "are you sure about us? I mean, letting people know?"

A light purring rose through the floor as the furnace in the basement kicked on to maintain the temperature at a comfortable level. The curtains drawn across the window fluttered in the warm air gusting from the vent in the floor. I glanced sideways at Sue. In the steady light from the candles on the dresser and nightstands, I saw that her face had gone rigid and her eyes, full of water, were glaring at the ceiling.

"Okay," I said. "Never mind. When your friend gets back from the Dominican we'll have our drink and figure out what to do about your parents. Now, since we've decided to be reckless, how about a spin in the Chevy?"

She closed her eyes, blinked away the tears. Smiling, she stretched her arms and her legs until they were so taut they trembled.

IT WAS LATE, blustery, the light of the street lamps dulled by the heavy air. In the streets of the neighbourhood only porch lights were on.

The car was a marvel, easy to handle, solid and smooth

on the pavement. The steering wheel was a little stiff but the pedals worked with oiled precision. The engine thrummed confidently. The headlights were hardly more powerful than a couple of weak flashlights but, with no one around, wandering cats and prowling raccoons would be the only danger. I was surprised at its speed, its responsiveness.

Sue marvelled at the job I'd done. She said, thinking of the gathering where we'd met, that I would win prizes.

"Thanks." But I'd been only half-listening, her words, her enthusiasm reaching me through a growing sense of dread. It was as if my very flesh was beginning to revolt. I said, "Sue, this can't go on."

"What are you talking about?" Her voice had an unhappy edge.

"This. Us."

She twisted around in the seat to face me. "What are you saying?"

"I'm saying that I can't do what you want to do. I have too much to lose."

"To lose? *You* have a lot to lose? What do *you* have to lose?"

"Everything."

She steadied herself with a hand on the dashboard, took a deep breath. Suddenly subdued, she said, "Don't be a bastard, Alec. Tell me what you're talking about."

That's when I knew, with utter certainty, that I was trapped.

"Tell me."

Tell her? Why not? She held in her palm my entire world, everything I'd worked for, everything I'd built. She merely had to make a fist to crush it all. Reputations are like spiders' webs, a wave of the hand is all it takes. Whether she learned the truth or not was irrelevant. She'd gone much further than I had in this adventure and she wouldn't let it be, of that I was sure. She would have her revenge. I would become a source of outrage and betrayal for much of my clientele and, even worse, be turned into a laughingstock, a figure of ridicule, in the industry.

More calmly than I would ever have imagined, I said, "Sue, this might come as a bit of a shock but my name's not Alec and I'm not a house painter."

In the seat beside me, her body went rigid. I should have turned right at the next corner in order to remain in my neighbourhood but I chose not to, chose instead to continue heading north towards an area where the streets were more heavily treed with evergreens, where the lots were more extensive, where the houses were larger and set farther back from the road, sometimes behind stone fences and locked gates.

As I drove, I revealed all to Sue, beginning with my real name. I left out nothing: my parents, my inheritance, my company, my persona. I told her about the hotel rooms and the girls from the agency, about my arrival at the Den and about her friend Kelly.

She remained silent through it all, uttering not a sound, hardly seeming to breathe.

As I spoke, a curious feeling grew in me — a sense of lightness, almost of joy. My words were peeling back layer upon layer of fabrication, getting closer with each new detail to another me, one I thought I'd left behind, the me who began seeing ways of renovating my bedroom in my parents' house, the me who had cheap business cards printed up to give to clients of the hardware store, the me who believed there was no price to be paid for what were merely creative means to a financial end. This was a me I hadn't encountered in years.

From the feeling it brought — a kind of giddying liberation, perhaps? — and from Sue's silence as well, a hope began to grow, a hope so far-fetched, so fantastical that later it would come to seem like the delusions of a foolish man. I thought it likely that, fully appraised of the situation, she would understand and accept my need for secrecy and would continue, despite everything, being my partner in crime. It was with an expectation of acquiescence that I said, "So you see, Sue, I can't afford ... Well, I guess I just can't afford to have you in my life publicly. You get it, don't you? So it'd be better if we just —"

Aware only of the effect my words were having on me, heedless of the effect they were having on her, I was stunned when she began emitting a strange, low keening sound. On the seat beside me, her silhouette was doubled over, her fists pressed to her forehead.

"Sue?"

The keening intensified, filling the car.

I pulled over to the curb, the weak headlights briefly illuminating a stone wall, and reached a hand out to her arm. She recoiled, pressing herself hard against the passenger door.

"Don't touch me." Her voice was low, a growled whisper.

I withdrew my hand.

"You've been lying to me all along."

"You're a fine one to talk about lying. You've been lying to your parents all along."

"You son-of a-bitch."

Hands scrabbling at the latch, she shoved the car door open. Cool air surged in as she tumbled out.

This was too much. She was being unreasonable, overly dramatic. "Sue!" I called. "What do you think you're doing?"

Paying no attention to me, she slammed the door shut and began running, a wild and ghostly figure in my headlights fleeing through the dark, deserted street, the habitat most natural to her.

I put the car into gear, followed her as she ran, stumbled, ran again. The car drew close. She turned towards me, her face contorted into an ugliness that made her unrecognizable, those centimetres that had fallen in her favour shoved out of alignment by a depth of rage I could never hope to soothe.

I braked, Sue — brown-skinned, dark-haired, dark-eyed Sue — lined up in the headlights not ten feet away.

APPEARANCES ARE DECEIVING. So what else is new? The cliché even applies to things. Outwardly, my garage was as it had always been — spacious, well-lit, tools neatly shelved, not an oil stain on the cement floor. Only now, its nature had changed, by necessity. From a place dedicated to making the old new again, it had turned into a chop shop.

I rolled the acetylene tank close to the Chevy, checked the gauge. It was almost full. I twisted the valve open, held up the flame of the cigarette lighter to the hiss of gas. The *whomp* and *whoosh* of the flame excited something in me. It's an unruly beast, fire. Uncontained, it eats ravenously, without discrimination, cremating men alive, incinerating the world. But scaled back, trimmed to the blue blade bristling from the mouth of the spout, it becomes domesticated, obedient, a split atom held in the fist.

Regret, sentimentality: I've never been partial to such pointless self-indulgence. Still, not dwelling on the hours of effort I'd lavished on the car and the beauty I'd achieved took a little effort. I expected the first cut would be the hardest, harder even than the thorough dismantling the car had already undergone. Removing the seats and stripping them into unrecognizable junk had taken hardly more than a couple of hours. The doors and wheels lay stacked in a corner beside the engine which hung from its tripod like some massive, blackened heart spouting valves and ventricles and dangling rubber arteries. Extracting the windshield, the headlights, the wooden ribs I'd so carefully wrought, unscrewing every removable part, then cutting and smashing them all had taken rather longer. But all those parts could be replaced, the destruction reversed, a thought that sat at the back of my mind as I laboured.

Now though, the irreparable was at hand.

I ran my palm along the hood, wondering where to apply the hissing flame. Was there a technique to carving a car as there was to a turkey? The metal was warm to the touch and it was that warmth, I think, that summoned the memory of Sue draping herself on the car, her dress hitched up around her waist. I imagined there would be moments when I would miss her — not quite the right verb, too intense, but it will have to do. After all, we were alike in so many ways, more ways than I'd suspected.

The news had reported it as a hit-and-run. There had been no witnesses. The papers ran photos of her parents' house, a food van parked in the driveway. On TV, a friend of the family, a Mr. Kumar, called on the police to do all they could to apprehend the guilty party. She was an only child, he said, and whoever had done this had killed three people. From the news reports, I learned that Sue was really Sumintra and that she'd lived with her parents in the suburbs.

I held the flame to the hood. The paint darkened and crinkled in the heat. With a slow hand, feeling a kind of admiration for the game she'd played, I let the flame trace the silhouette of a sprawled human body: the torso, the arms, the hands, the head. My fear of that first cut proved unfounded.

I'd never registered the car so, for all intents and purposes, it's never existed. The bits and pieces will trickle out with my regular garbage, household detritus. The pieces of wooden frame might make good firewood. The larger metal pieces to which the frame will eventually be reduced I will dump here and there throughout the countryside next summer during my weekend trips in search of antiques.

I'VE ALWAYS ADMIRED the Roman Catholic ritual of confession. As I understand it, you reveal your secret sins to someone who will forgive you for them but can't do anything *with* them. In practical terms, it's as if you haven't told anyone but you still get the thrill of *telling*. Because that's the best thing about secrets: the thrill of sharing an entertaining tale with a stranger who wields no power over you. Everyone benefits in his own way. After all, now that I've told you my secrets, don't you feel better about yours?